Margaret Majendie

Precautions

A novel. Part 2

Margaret Majendie

Precautions
A novel. Part 2

ISBN/EAN: 9783337051099

Printed in Europe, USA, Canada, Australia, Japan

Cover: Foto ©Andreas Hilbeck / pixelio.de

More available books at **www.hansebooks.com**

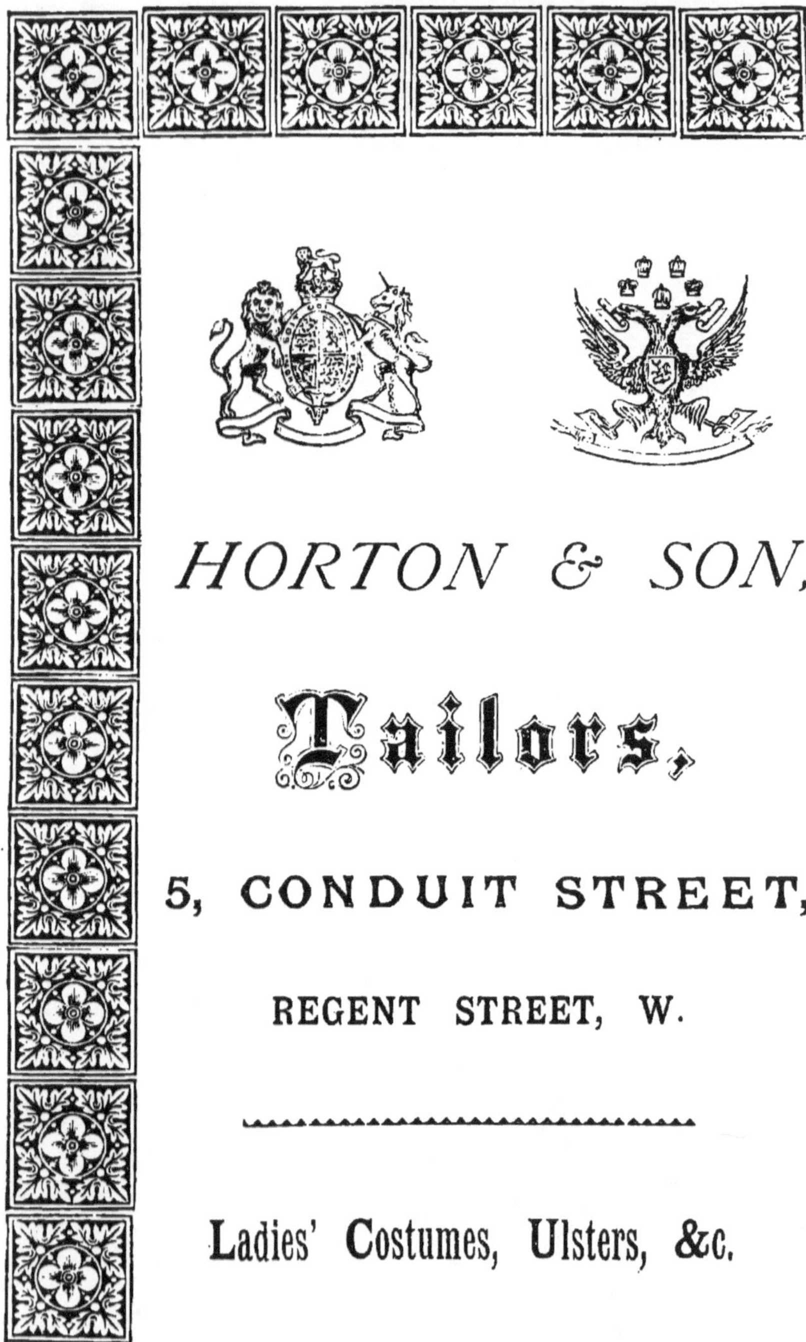

HORTON & SON,

Tailors,

5, CONDUIT STREET,

REGENT STREET, W.

Ladies' Costumes, Ulsters, &c.

COOK & HOLDWAY,

Coachbuilders by Special Appointment to Her Majesty,

MOUNT STREET, GROSVENOR SQUARE.

Estimates for repairs, on town or country examinations, furnished free.

Any Carriage jobbed with the option of purchase on favourable terms.

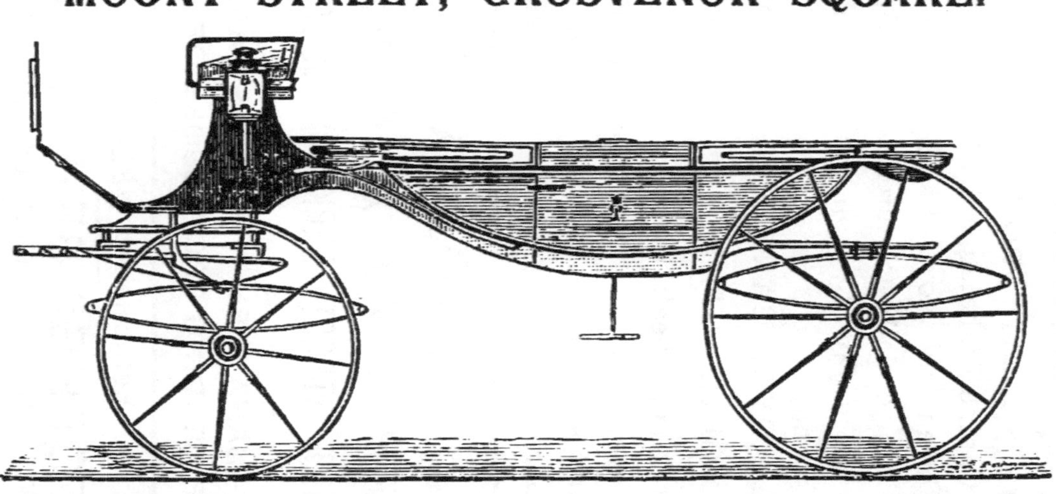

LANDAUS in all sizes with balanced heads, and one-horse Landaus specially light of draught.

BROUGHAMS of which Cook & Holdway were the Inventors and original Builders (for Lord Brougham) in three sizes.

SOCIABLE VICTORIAS, with or without doors, for one horse or a pair.   New design.

TO CONNOISSEURS AND INVALIDS.

THE PRINCE'S PORT,

50 YEARS IN WOOD.

PALE COLOR.   SOFT.   DELICATE.

Eminent authorities recommend this <u>*PORT*</u>, *well* <u>*matured in Wood*</u>, *not only for general consumption, but especially for the use of those suffering from gout.*

In Portugal, where gout is unknown, this style of Port is always used.

BERRY BROS. & Co.,

3, ST. JAMES'S STREET,

LONDON, S.W.

ESTABLISHED 200 YEARS.

A detailed price-list of Wines, Spirits, and Liqueurs on application

TIME - SAVING PUBLICATIONS.

			s.	d.
Account Books	..	from	1	0
Bills Paid Books	..	..	3	6
Cellar Books	..	..	1	6
,, ,,	..	..	9	6
Daily Consumption Books	..		4	6
,, ,, ,,		..	10	6
Dairy Account Books		..	8	6
Engagement Books	..		1	6
,, ,,	..		2	6
Game Books	..		2	6
,, ,,			4	6
,, ,,			6	6
,, ,,			12	0
,, ,,	..	..	21	0
Horse Registers	..	..	15	0
Household Account Books		..	1	0
,, ,, ,,	..	..	5	0
,, ,, ,,	..		6	6
,, Inventory Books	..	..	2	0
,, Washing Books	..	..	1	0
Larder Books	..		1	6
Linen Books	..	..	6	6
Menu Books	..	..	4	0
Poultry Account Books	..		2	0
Stable Expenses Books		..	2	6
Visiting Books	..	..	4	0
,, ,,	..	..	5	0
Wages Books (Servant's)			3	6
,, ,, ,,		..	5	6
Wine Bin Books	..	..	3	6

J. DAY & SON,

PUBLISHERS & BOOKSELLERS,

16, MOUNT STREET, W.

A more useful present could not possibly be selected than one of A. H. WOODWARD'S "HALL MARKED" SILVER I.X.L. PENCIL CASES. Those below are the most saleable designs. See that the Trade Marks A.H.W. & I.X.L. are stamped on the point and have no other.

No. 424 S.	 Double-Action Spiral Pencil, for Watch Chain, Richly Engraved.	6/- EACH
425 S.	 Double-Action Spiral Pencil, Richly Engraved.	6/- EACH
586.	 Ivory Pencil Case, with Hall-Marked Silver Double-Action Movements, nicely Engine-cut or Damask'd.	7/6 EACH
648 S.	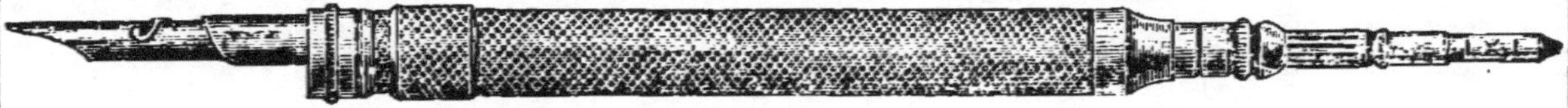 Sliding Penholder and Single Spiral Pencil, nicely Engine-cut, very useful.	7/6 EACH
585	 Extra-strong Hall-Marked Sterling Silver Elongated Penholder and Spiral Pencil combined, with Reserve of Leads. Open 7-inches, Closed 3¼-inches. The most useful Pen and Pencil Case made.	10/6 EACH

I.X.L. WORKS, VITTORIA STREET, BIRMINGHAM, & 1, FOSTER LANE, LONDON, E.C.

Sold by JOHN DAY & SON, 16 Mount St., Grosvenor Sq., W., and all respectable Stationers.

SWEDISH NOTE PAPER.

SWEDISH NOTE PAPER.

SWEDISH NOTE PAPER.

SWEDISH NOTE PAPER.

SWEDISH NOTE PAPER.

SWEDISH NOTE PAPER.

SWEDISH NOTE PAPER.

SWEDISH NOTE PAPER.

Samples may be had post free on application.

JOHN DAY & SON,

Stationers,

HENNIG BROS.,

New and Second-hand

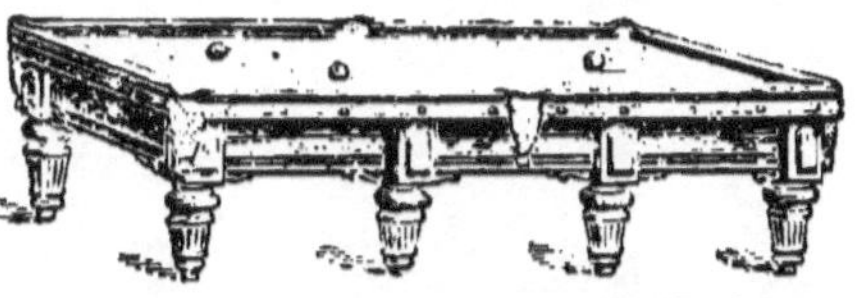

BILLIARD and **BAGATELLE TABLES,**

In all Sizes and at all Prices.

BILLIARD BALLS,
CLOTHS, CHALKS, CUES, TIPS,

And all other Billiard Requisites.

WHOLESALE, RETAIL, & FOR EXPORTATION.

OLD BALLS ADJUSTED OR EXCHANGED,

AND

TABLES RE-CUSHIONED and RE-COVERED,

Adjusted, Removed, Bought, Sold, or Warehoused,

And every kind of Billiard Work executed with dispatch & at moderate charges.

Price Lists, Cloth and Cushion Rubber Samples, Post Free.

When writing for Samples of the latter, please state for what kind of Table they are wanted.

HENNIG BROS.,

BILLIARD TABLE MAKERS,

11, HIGH ST., LONDON, W.C.

(Opposite St. Giles's Church.)

ESTABLISHED 1862.

Mr. JOHN D. WOOD,

AGENT FOR

WEST-END HOUSES,
COUNTRY HOUSES,
SUMMER and RIVERSIDE HOUSES,
SHOOTINGS and FISHINGS,
HUNTING BOXES,
YACHTING HOUSES.

Offices—19, MOUNT ST., LONDON, W.

A Novel.

BY

LADY MARGARET MAJENDIE,

AUTHOR OF

'FASCINATION,' 'SISTERS-IN-LAW,' 'THE TURN OF THE TIDE,' ETC.

IN THREE VOLUMES.

VOL. III.

LONDON:

RICHARD BENTLEY AND SON,

Publishers in Ordinary to Her Majesty the Queen.

1887.

PRECAUTIONS.

CHAPTER I.

THE morning was very fine; all the tall French windows were set wide open, the table drawn so close to them that the hanging roses outside and the gathered ones within made it seem a bower of flowers.

Kitty came down late. She looked white and exhausted; the heat oppressed her. Alice had already fulfilled her duties, and poured out the tea.

'You are late, Kitty,' she exclaimed

gaily.; 'so I have been doing all your work.'

'You should not be so late, Kitty,' said Mrs. Brown-Clifford. 'What would your aunt have said in old days if you had not been in your place when the bell rang?'

'*Nous avons changé tout cela,*' said Eustace lazily, and Kitty's timid look at him was full of gratitude. He brought her all she wanted. As his love failed, his careful consideration for her increased tenfold.

The newspapers always arrived at breakfast-time; they were brought in now.

When Kitty began her breakfast, Lady Bellingham obtained her invariable second cup of tea, and Mrs. Brown-Clifford drew her knitting from her bag. Eustace unfolded one paper, and handed another to his brother-in-law.

Alice drew her chair nearer to the window, and began to feed a little Italian greyhound which was a pet of Kitty's. It was a shivery little thing, with some of the dainty timidity of its mistress, fastidious over its saucer of cream, which it began, interrupting itself every moment to look up at Alice with alarmed eyes.

Presently Georgie gave a great start. She was looking at her husband.

'What is the matter, Joe?' she exclaimed. 'Is there any bad news in the paper?'

He cleared his throat loudly.

'Bad news? What an idea! You are very imaginative, Georgie.' He rapidly folded up the paper, and exclaimed, 'What, all finished breakfast! Give me an egg, Georgie.'

'They are cold now,' she said, still watching him.

But he took it, broke the shell, began, and put it aside.

'What a stifling morning!' he said. 'Have you done, Kitty? What do you say—shall we go out at once?'

Lady Bellingham looked at him with astonishment; and Alice said, laughing:

'If you are thirsting for a cigar, Joe, do not wait for us. It is much too hot to go out yet.'

Joseph Mulroy laid his hand heavily on his brother-in-law's shoulder.

'Come out, Eustace,' he said.

Eustace's face was concealed by the paper. He started and rose to his feet.

'Come out, Eustace,' repeated Joe mechanically.

Eustace shook off his hand. He was very white, his face set hard. Kitty saw it with sudden terror. She clasped her hands, and looked up at him with frightened eyes.

' It is very hot,' he stammered.

' Yes; come with me, Eustace,' and again he touched his arm.

Eustace turned round to his wife, trying to force a smile.

' You will excuse me, Kitty. You see, Joe is so ardent a smoker that he cannot be restrained.'

' There is some bad news in the paper,' said Mrs. Brown-Clifford composedly, as the two men disappeared through the open window. ' The best thing we can do is to look for ourselves, and get to the root of the matter.'

She folded up her knitting, and took up the paper that had fallen to the ground. It was one of the Society papers, and in its columns was a detailed account of the strange marriage ceremony which had taken place between Lord Austen and his cousin Marion by the death-bed of her father. The story was told with dramatic force.

Mrs. Clifford read it to the end without comment. Kitty came quietly forward, and read over her shoulder. Then she stood for a moment, the room reeling round her, with both her hands clinging for support to the back of her mother's chair.

The first sensation was one of the extremest happiness. Marion was married! Would not this be the one thing that would give her the undivided love of her own husband? Then cold with a sudden chill swept across her the sight of Eustace's stricken face.

She reeled slightly; she would have done so more, but her mother turned half round, put her arm round her, and held her firmly, casting looks that could only mean defiance on all about her.

Alice, who had also hastily glanced at

the paper, saw this look. A kind of hostility
burnt in her breast. She saw not Kitty's
white face and little convulsive hands
struggling against the deadly faintness that
was stealing over her senses ; she only saw
in her the woman who she thought had
wrecked her brother's happiness.

‘ I do not see why you should look as if
some great misfortune had happened,' she
said bitterly. ‘ Surely, Kitty, this news
should be welcome to you.'

‘ I do not see that,' said Mrs. Brown-
Clifford ; ‘ on the contrary, it ought to be a
matter of profound indifference to her, to
you, and to your brother.'

‘ You cannot expect us to see it in the
same light,' said Lady Bellingham, trying
to speak with polite ease. ‘ To me this
news is quite delightful. It puts an end
to many anxieties respecting my dear
niece's future ; it ensures her happiness,

Altogether, I shall claim your congratulations.'

'Your son ought to be ashamed of himself,' said Mrs. Brown-Clifford.

It was as if a thunderbolt had fallen in their midst. This dreadful old woman was quite capable of putting into words all that for so long they had so studiously laboured to ignore—all but Alice. Alice had never ceased to resent Eustace's marriage. Only conventionalities had held her silent. The breaking down of the barrier seemed to her almost a relief.

'You dare not repeat such words of my brother!' she said haughtily.

'Hoity-toity!' exclaimed Mrs. Brown-Clifford. 'Dare! That is a strong word, young lady.'

'Mamma, mamma!' panted poor Kitty.

But Mrs. Brown-Clifford only led her towards the door.

'Go to your room, Kitty,' she said, 'and stay there. The time has come which I have long seen approaching, and I must have it out with these women.'

Kitty knew how useless it was for her to offer the smallest opposition to her inexorable parent. In an agony of fear and shame, she fled away along the passages, striving to shut out all sounds from her ears.

Mrs. Brown-Clifford went back to the dining-room table and sat down.

'Now we will have it out,' she said grimly.

Lady Bellingham spoke first.

'Mrs. Clifford,' she said with a forced laugh, 'you remind me of Don Quixote tilting with the windmills. Would it not be better to let us go on in our perpetual round?'

'Grinding hearts into flour.'

Alice started forward indignantly.

'What are you aiming at?' she exclaimed. 'What is it that you wish to insinuate?'

'Nothing at all. I only speak in the plainest Queen's English. Between you all you have broken my daughter's heart.'

'You exaggerate in the strangest way,' said Lady Bellingham. 'Kitty's complaints must proceed from her own imagination. Many young wives are exacting.'

'Kitty never complains.'

'Then, pardon me, it is a little difficult to understand.'

'None so blind as those that won't see. Why, your son's face, when he read that news this morning, was the face of a man who had received a mortal blow; and I defy you to deny it!'

'This is intolerable!' exclaimed Alice.

'Intolerable, you call it? You are not far wrong there. It is so intolerable that

the time has come for her mother's in-
terference.'

'I cannot see what fault you can find
with my son,' said Lady Bellingham. 'His
conduct to his wife has been exemplary;
if you wish to make it otherwise, you have
only to pursue the course you have now
entered upon.'

'Why did he look like that?'

'Why?' exclaimed Alice vehemently.
'I think you are the very last person in the
world who should ask why. Because he saw
in this paper the saddest story you could
wish to see—the forced marriage of the
woman he once loved to a man whom she
cannot love—detailed in it, and he pitied
her fate.'

'You jump to conclusions, and you mis-
calculate the mixed motives that actuate
people's actions!' exclaimed Mrs. Clifford.
'Why do you calumniate your friend?

Why do you assume that she does not love her husband?'

'We need not enter into the question of her feelings,' said Alice haughtily.

'You yourself began it. Is that the only reason that Eustace turned whiter than snow, and looked as he did just now—because he pitied the girl who in following his own example made as good a match as he did himself? Nonsense!'

Alice was so angry that she forgot herself. She spoke calmly, but she said words she ought never to have uttered.

'You know better than I do how the whole thing was brought about. You accuse my brother of mercenary motives in his marriage, and I emphatically deny them.'

Mrs. Brown-Clifford gave one of her significant snorts. Lady Bellingham came forward and caught hold of Alice's hand.

' Alice, Alice!' she exclaimed ; ' take care what you say.'

But Alice would not listen.

' I will not be silent,' she said, ' and hear Eustace accused of dishonourable conduct. You yourself, mamma, know better ; and in case Mrs. Clifford does not choose to know, I will repeat it. Eustace married Kitty solely and entirely out of compassion, because he was told distinctly that she was pining away because she cared for him, and he would not let another suffer what he was bearing with such heroism : that was the conduct of my noble, generous brother. Kitty has had what she wanted ; she knew his whole story, and if she is not satisfied it is——'

The words died away on her lips. There, just within the door, clinging to the handle, white, and trembling from head to foot, stood little Kitty. She must have heard every word.

She came forward into the room, turning from one to another, her hands clasped, with a look of agonized entreaty, and her voice was almost shrill as she cried :

'Alice ! tell me it is not true ! Mother, mother ! Lady Bellingham ! tell me that it is not true !'

There was no answer. What could they say ?

Alice was horror-stricken at the effect of her own words ; she would have given all she possessed for the power of unsaying them. The agony in Kitty's face haunted her for many a long day afterwards.

Kitty, looking from one to another, fancied she only read compassion in their downcast faces. A cry that was half-moan, halfwail, burst from her lips.

'Oh, mother !—Alice ! I am ashamed—

I am ashamed! What shall I do?' she cried.

Georgie came forward suddenly, speaking abruptly.

'All that you have to do, Kitty, is to forget all that you have heard, and that has been said. Never mind how your marriage was brought about, or motives one way or another. You and Eustace belong to each other; nothing can do away with that, thank God!'

But Kitty did not seem to hear her. She put both her hands to her temples, thrusting them into the fair dishevelled hair, and she went away so, out of the room, down the passage. They could hear the little moans of anguish, wrung from her as she went, all the way to her own room; then the closing and locking of the door.

The others looked at each other awe-stricken. It was too serious now to resume the angry conversation. Alice went away in bitter tears of sorrow and repentance for her hasty words ; the other ladies talked in whispers, almost friends in their mutual anxiety about the poor young wife.

CHAPTER II.

THE morning passed on leaden wings; it seemed as if the hours would never pass.

Alice, in her own room, worked herself up into a frenzy of misery about her brother. He had always been the idol of her life, his happiness her first and principal thought. She fancied that he must be suffering cruelly ; she was unnerved by all that had taken place, and everything jarred upon her. At luncheon, it was almost a shock when Eustace came in, looking absolutely the same as usual—perhaps rather more than usually bright and alert—after a long walk with his brother-in-law through woods and new plantations. He spoke with interest, and was full of outdoor plans and improvements. Alice, in the revulsion of feeling, thought him heartless. She could not understand it.

He asked for Kitty, but a servant had brought a message that she had a bad headache, and begged not to be disturbed; he expressed himself not satisfied, and, leaving his untasted luncheon, went off to her boudoir.

Alice looked after him with the strange perverse feeling in her heart that he was neither faithful nor true; she could not have put it into words, but to see his trouble cured was grief, not pleasure, to her.

Eustace went to his wife's room, and entered very softly. She was lying back in a large armchair, in her soft pale-blue gown, her hair pushed back, her eyes closed, her whole attitude sad and dispirited. He came close to her, kneeling on one knee, and taking her little cold hands in his :

' Kitty dear,' he said gently, ' are you in pain ?'

She looked up at him, reading nothing in his eyes but a look of kind compassion. She saw nothing more there—nothing of the great tenderness of strength for the fragile and weak that was welling up in his breast—nothing of that protecting affection that has something of a father's instinct in it, which made him feel that this little wife of his needed all his strength and care, and that this fact of her great need of him was opening to her the great store of love that had been closed against her while he only thought of himself.

All this was a sealed book to her. She read only the pity from which she shrank with a kind of terror, because she had learned so rudely that the whole sacrifice of his life and happiness was due to that, and that her love for him had proved his very bane.

Kitty felt the clasp of his hands, and looked up into his face—that face that seemed to her the noblest, handsomest on earth; she laid her head down for a moment on his breast; she clasped her arms round his neck, and held him fast.

'Kitty,' he repeated, 'are you suffering, dear?'

But she could not answer; the words would have choked her; the terrible pain in the throat stopped their utterance. He only saw the drawn look of suffering on her white forehead, and thought it physical.

'Poor child! poor little thing!' he said tenderly.

He rearranged her pillows, he closed the blinds, then came back and stood beside her lingeringly.

' I had better leave you in peace, dear?' he said ; and she answered whisperingly, ' Yes. Go—go!'

He stooped down and kissed her brow ; still under the same impression, she shrank away a little from his kiss. Then he went away, pausing to look back, and haunted by some look in her eyes that he had never seen before—a look so wistful, so piteous, that he felt a sudden pang of fear at his heart, not knowing what it meant.

Kitty sent word by her maid that no one was to disturb her until she rang her bell, so that they fancied she hoped to sleep ; and the others arranged their own plans for the afternoon.

Five o'clock came, and she did not appear. Gathering round the tea-table,

they congratulated themselves on the length
and quiet of her rest.

At seven o'clock, Eustace came in again
and asked for his wife, still learning that
she had not rung, and must not be disturbed.

The time passed on ; they all met at
dinner, and in the midst of it Eustace rose
up and said that, in spite of his wife's wish,
he should take up some soup for her—she
had eaten nothing since breakfast. Alice
said that she thought Kitty would rather
not be disturbed ; but he only frowned
slightly, and said that it was not good for
her.   And he went upstairs.

Some time passed ; the conversation
dragged, the dinner seemed tasteless and
bad ; only Mrs. Brown-Clifford, whose appe-
tite never flagged, plodded slowly on
through course after course. No one quite
knew why this gloom had fallen upon them,

but it seemed as if trouble were in the air, and as if there were nothing unexpected in the long delay, and in the curious look on Eustace's face when he did return.

'Kitty must have gone out,' he said, speaking hoarsely. 'Did anyone know of her intention? She is not in her room.'

'She must be in the garden,' said Georgie. 'She often sits there after dinner.'

'She is not in the garden—I have looked. Did she say that she was going out? Alice, what is the matter? Why do you look so pale?'

'Nothing; I am all right,' answered Alice.

She was trying to control her trembling limbs; a deadly fear was in her mind. She saw the others glance at her, and, as if in a dream, she saw the look in Eustace's face suddenly growing suspicious.

'What is the matter?' he exclaimed, looking at the conscious faces. 'What have you been doing to my wife?' He caught hold of his mother's hand. 'You, at least, never scruple to tell me plain unvarnished truth!' he exclaimed. 'Tell me why you all look like that, mother!'

Mrs. Brown-Clifford broke the silence.

'Why, because if your wife is missing, if you find her lying at the bottom of the lake, you have only to thank yourselves for it!' she exclaimed.

'Do not speak like that!' cried Joseph Mulroy loudly. 'It is all nonsense! Why do we linger like this? let us go and find her.'

'It is all Alice's fault, Eustace,' cried Lady Bellingham, 'so do not look at me. Alice told her why you married her.'

'I did not! I did not!' cried Alice passionately.

'No, no!' cried Georgie. 'Angry words were passing — unfortunately dear Kitty heard.'

'Heard what? What did you say?' he cried, turning fiercely upon his sister.

Alice was desperate.

'I told nothing but the truth!' she exclaimed; 'that you married her out of compassion for her love of you.'

For one moment his head sank on his breast.

'My poor little wife!'

Then he pushed aside the hand Alice laid on his shoulder; with a violent effort he suppressed the passionate reproaches that rose to his lips, and mastering himself, spoke with rapid decision.

'Mulroy, will you come with me? There will be matters to arrange. Mother, will you kindly order some dinner to be kept hot for Kitty when she comes in? Come, Joe.'

Alice, with a little faint cry, caught at his hand as he passed, but failed; he would not, could not, even look at her—the blow had been too keen.

Mrs. Brown-Clifford's voice followed them shrilly.

'Have the lake dragged, Sir Eustace!'

Once outside the door, Eustace's firmness for one instant gave way to terror.

'Joe!' he exclaimed, grasping him with painful force; 'this will have killed her.'

'No, no! a thousand times no! Kitty is as good as an angel.'

A thought of Kitty's goodness; of her loving, gentle faith; of the little set phrases, almost like maxims, that she sometimes used to express the good and holy thoughts that passed through her mind — all this flashed through his brain. They had wearied him in his selfish clinging to that which was gone, but now it came back to him with a flash of hope that Kitty was very good—she would have strength to suffer and to bear.

He groaned aloud.

'What shall we do? How shall we set to work, Joe?' he said.

Before Mr. Mulroy could answer, some one came running up to them in the hall. It was Kitty's maid—her eyes red with weeping. She held a letter in her hand.

'Sir Eustace, a boy has just brought this. He says her ladyship gave it to him at the station, and that she went up to London by the four o'clock train.'

Joseph Mulroy looked the congratulations he could not utter as the maid went lingeringly away. He opened the door of the billiard-room, and they went in. He hesitated whether he should leave his brother-in-law to read the letter alone; but a glance at his ashy face made him resolve not to do so.   He went away to a distant window, and stood there waiting.

There was a long silence.   Then Joseph turned round.   Sir Eustace had thrown himself into a chair and covered his face with one hand ; the other was extended on a table, the letter crumpled in it.

' She is all right, old fellow, eh ?' said Joe, trying to speak cheerily.

Eustace tossed the letter towards him.

' Am I to read it ?' he said hesitatingly.

' Yes, read it.   For her sake, the more publicity that it has the better,' he answered bitterly.   ' She is so young, so utterly in-experienced ; she little knows what she has done.'

' But does she give no address? Of course we must find her at once, and set this miserable misunderstanding right,' he said eagerly.

Eustace only made a quick gesture, and he took up the letter and read :

'Dear, dear Eustace,

'I have learnt the truth at last ; but I want you to believe that I did not know it, that if I had had even the smallest suspicion that you wished to marry me out of compassion I would never have done it. I could not have accepted such a sacrifice. I am so sorry—so very sorry. I thought you asked me because I could be a comfort to you, and because you could some day learn to love me. But now I know the truth I hardly know how to bear it.

'Darling, I cannot undo the fatal knot that binds you to me. I cannot set you free ; but at least I can remove myself out of your way, and then you will be more at ease again. And my greatest happiness would be to know that you had returned to your old peaceful life without the burden of a wife you cannot love, and then you can forget me. Do forget me, darling ! Shut me away out of your life as if I had never been ; and try to be happy again. Do not look for me—let me go. I want to go and hide away my sorrow, and try to forget that my love has proved so terrible a misfortune to you. I would free you if I could, but my life belongs to God.

'Darling, I did not know—believe me that I did not know—or I would never, never have been your wife.

'KITTY.'

Joe Mulroy's eyes were blinded with tears as he laid the letter down.

'What do you mean to do ?' he said earnestly.

'Do ! Move heaven and earth to find her, and to prove to her——'

He stopped. Joe put his hand upon his shoulder.

'If you have no love to give her, Eustace,' he said, 'in mercy to her would it not be best to let her be ?'

Eustace made an impatient gesture.

'Love, love !' he exclaimed. 'It is always the same jargon. It is not like May. A man can only love like that once in his life; but this is different.'

'Yes,' said Joe eagerly; 'but can you convince her of that?'

'My poor little wife !' he exclaimed. 'How can I atone? What can I say?'

'A little love.'

'I don't know what you call love, Joe. Is it enough that I feel that I cannot live without her ?'

'She will come back. It will be all right,' said Joseph Mulroy hopefully.

CHAPTER III.

BUT the days and weeks went by, and Kitty did not come back. Eustace was not content to wait. He put the management of the search into the hands of private police; he spared neither time nor effort himself, but all with no result. It was a simple fact that, on that fatal day in July, young Lady Bellingham had gone up to London by a four o'clock train. Her maid said that she must have worn a simple black cachemire gown that was missing. On reaching London, who would have remarked a very quiet, slender little woman in black, who quickly walked away from the train and disappeared ? The detectives were baffled by the very simplicity of the thing, and were quite without a clue.

Eustace would not give up hope as the time passed; he continued the search with a feeling occasionally of absolute despair. Never had he even guessed for a moment how dear his little gentle wife had become to him. Remorse pressed painfully upon him for his deficiencies towards her. He longed to find her passionately, and to plead for forgiveness and reconciliation. He would not leave Castleford; he fancied that, if she ever changed her mind, she would come back there.

Lady Bellingham came and established herself with him, resuming her old duties as mistress of the house ; and Alice came with her. But Alice did not stay long. Do what he would to conceal it, Eustace could not forgive her ; it seemed to him that her cruel words had wilfully hunted Kitty away. Even her wistful, sorrowful looks did not soften him. He tried hard to be the same to her, but he could not. All the more for the unusual affection and confidence that had always existed between them did the revulsion of feeling strike him and make him hard.

Poor Alice suffered greatly. She had fancied herself his best friend—his truest and most faithful friend ; the only one who shared and kept up by her intense sympathy the constant remembrance of his old love for Marion. Now suddenly, and with agony, she had seen her conduct in its true light. She saw that little Kitty's faithful, gentle love might have won her husband had she had quite fair play, and (bitterest pang of all) she realized that Eustace had been fast learning to be consoled. In bitter tears she bemoaned her own conduct. Very timidly she tried to win back her position in her brother's confidence, but it was too soon; and feeling that she could not bear it, she left Castleford, and went to stay with the Mulroys in London.

Mrs. Brown-Clifford returned to Richmond. She took no alarm ; she had a strong conviction that Kitty would reappear some day, and meanwhile was not sorry that all her new family should be pretty severely punished, for they deserved it, in her opinion.

That the punishment was very severe no one could doubt who saw Eustace's thin, haggard face, from which all the light of youth seemed to have faded. She might even have pitied him.

The London season was drawing towards an end. The Mulroys had refused all invitations; in the condition of sorrow and suspense in which the family was plunged, they had neither heart nor inclination for gaiety. Alice also was an anxiety. Her courage and strength had alike given way; she suffered from painful fits of crying and subsequent prostration, and took no interest in anything.

Joseph Mulroy was kindness itself, but he was uncongenial to Alice. His views of art, the painting in which he delighted, and which Alice condemned as so unskilful— all gave her a feeling of contempt for him. Georgie saw it, she understood it thoroughly. She also had experienced it, but it was different now. She knew that her Joe was not clever; she knew that he was un-educated; that he was insignificant in appearance, and in no way a shining light; but what did that matter to her? He was her husband—first, foremost, all in all to her, and she resented the feelings she perceived in Alice, in spite of her strong efforts to conceal them. There was sorrow and bitterness among them all.

One day Joseph Mulroy came in with a brighter look than usual on his face.

'Who do you think I have seen?' he said eagerly.

Alice, who was lying reading listlessly on a sofa, looked up with so sudden a start of hope and expectation that good kind Joe bitterly reproached himself for his mode of announcement.

'No, no!' he exclaimed sorrowfully; 'not Kitty yet ; we must wait a little longer for that! It is our old acquaintance Ursel. He has come to London.'

Alice had sunk back wearily, and with indifference ; but Georgie, who had her very ugly, good-tempered baby on her knee, turned round beamingly :

'My dear Joe, that is good news. I do believe that that would please and interest Eustace.'

'I think Eustace would rather be left alone,' said Alice.

'No, I don't agree with you,' answered Georgie determinately. 'Staying on week after week at Castleford with mamma, as he is doing now, must be bad for him, especially as mamma is in the humour for telling home-truths all round ; and we all know what that means.'

'I am sure he would not leave home.'

'It would be a great gain to break through his miserable waiting there,' said Joe gently. 'I think you must think so too, Alice ; and if it would interest him to meet this man again, and perhaps to hear him play, it would be such a good thing.'

'I am the last person to consult about

Eustace's feelings or wishes,' said poor Alice. ' I know nothing of them now.'

Unwilling to notice her struggle with the tears that would come, Joe Mulroy took the crowing, kicking baby in his arms, and went on talking to Georgie.

' There is something peculiarly winning about Ursel. I feel the fascination almost as much as Eustace does, and I never saw any fellow so fascinated as he was.'

' Where did you meet him? What is he doing in London?'

' I met him at Novello's. He was buying fiddle-strings. You never saw anything so minute as his examination of each separate one. I believe he would have been hours over it if I had not come in. He jumped up and held out his hands with such a radiant look, and then the first thing was, Where was Eustace? and—all of you? But it is Eustace whom he likes so much.'

'Is he playing here? Why have we not heard of him? He must make a great sensation.'

'He is to play for the first time to-night. It is this wretched *impresario* who has brought him to London, and will pocket all his gains, clinging round him like an old man of the sea, so that he will make no fortune until his time is up.'

'Did you tell him about Eustace's loss?' said Alice, rather suddenly.

'No,' answered her brother-in-law. 'I saw no necessity for entering into particulars.'

'Where does he play?' asked Georgina.

'At St. James's Hall. Shall I try and get you places?'

'I should like it of all things, but——'

'Do not take one for me,' said Alice. 'I could not go.'

'Oh, then perhaps I had better not do so either.'

But Joseph Mulroy interposed. He wanted his wife to go. He thought it would do her good, and it was gloomy at home now. He could not help being conscious of Alice's feeling for him. His intuitive tact and insight were as sensitive as the needle to the pole, and though, in the beautiful humility of his character, he accepted it as a matter of course, and by no means a subject of resentment, yet in some way it weighed on and depressed his spirits.

'Come with me, Georgie,' he said, rather imploringly; and after that nothing would have prevented her from going.

Alice stayed at home, but she did not go to bed. She sat up till her sister and brother-in-law returned, very late, from St. James's Hall.

The effect of Ursel's playing had surpassed their wildest expectations. He had made a tremendous success.

'His fortune is made,' said Joe exultantly. 'I do not think anyone has been applauded so much since Paganini.'

'Did he play his best?'

'He was as long as usual tuning that one string; but then it was marvellous, as it always is. I did so long for Eustace to be here. He would have enjoyed his friend's triumph.'

'It is very late,' said Alice, stiffening at the mention of her brother's name.

She took her candle and went away to bed. The next day a persuasive note from Mr. Mulroy brought Ursel to luncheon.

The last two years had wrought some changes in the great *maestro*. He looked older, less simple, and there was an alteration in his dress and the manner of wearing it. Society had touched him with her civilizing finger. But in one respect he was quite the same. He still passed his hand through his fair bushy hair in moments of shyness or perplexity.

He asked eagerly after Eustace, and was much disappointed when he heard that he was not in London. His next question, about his friend's young wife, was more difficult to answer. They looked at each other with embarrassment, and Joe began, with much hesitation:

'Unfortunately there has been a slight misunderstanding.'

Ursel looked up with a start. Alice's cheeks were scarlet, her lips quivering. She took up the story herself.

'My brother's wife has left him, Herr Ursel,' she said.

He looked puzzled and grieved, but made no remark beyond a little bow and a short 'Ah! so?'

The visit was rather a failure. Mulroy had not the power of drawing out Ursel's strange charm, and neither Georgie nor Alice took part in the conversation. When he was going away Ursel said to his host :

'To-morrow, and next day, and Friday I play ; on Saturday I am free. Would it be allowed, do you think, that I should go down to Castleford?'

'My brother-in-law would, I know, be glad to see you; I am sure of it,' said Joe emphatically.

'I will carry my welcome with me. I will take Melusina ; she soothes trouble as David's harp soothed Saul. And he is in trouble—is it not so?'

'In bitter trouble,' answered Joe Mulroy.

'So.'

The answer was very simple.

On the following Saturday Ursel, carrying his violin-case in his hand, quietly walked up to the door at Castleford.

Sir Eustace was not at home, but he was

told that he would soon return, and left in the smoking-room.

When Eustace came in tired and dispirited, the first sound he heard was the wonderful tones of Melusina. He recognised them at once, and with one bound found himself in the presence of the musician. Ursel broke off suddenly, and came forward to meet him.

'Two years since we met,' he said in those quiet tones which took away from the abruptness of his words. 'Much has happened since then.'

'To you it has been one unbroken ascent up the ladder of success. Is it not so?'

'Yes ; but I also have suffered.'

'Madame Ursel ?'

The musician turned away his face; the light fell on his steady blue eyes.

'Yes,' he said gravely; 'my wife is dead.'

'Dead ! my poor friend! This is indeed unexpected.'

'I was very sorry,' he said. 'Poor Assunta! I was very fond of her. She did not love the violin ; our thoughts and ideas were not one, but she was young and very happy.'

'It is sad for the young and happy to die.'

'Do you think so? Not for them. Better to die in the glory of life than to fade in its shadow. She was gentle, she was innocent; she is in Paradise.'

'And you, my friend?'

'I have learnt a truer, loftier happiness in the exercise and perfection of my art.'

'Then you do not suffer now ?'

'My suffering has taught me passion. Melusina interprets it to the world. No great result can be produced without pain. You cannot call my playing cold now ?'

'Cold ! Did I ever think it cold?'

'I have improved,' said Ursel quietly.

'I will play to you ; I will play on your heart-strings as I used to do, shall I not ?'

'Not yet, not now ; in a few minutes. You know my trouble ?   There are wounds worse than death.'

'No, you mistake.   All other troubles bear in them the germ of future hope. Death only is irremediable, inexorable, and for which there is found no help.'

'You !   What do you know of life or death or sorrow ?' exclaimed Eustace passionately.   'You have never lived, you have never loved—you exist in the world of imagination ; your woes are fictitious, your joys and griefs bodiless as the music which represents your soul !'

Ursel looked thoughtful.

'Am I not mortal too?' he said.

'Not yet,' answered Eustace ; 'it is still to come.   Poor Assunta, poor pretty little soul!   Did it grieve her to leave you ?'

'I do not know,' said Ursel, a troubled look passing over his face ; 'it would have grieved her more if they had not laid her little dead baby on her breast, and told her they were going together.'

' Ah !' said Eustace.

He could say no more. He remembered the bright, foolish little wife with pain, and it seemed to him that Ursel, in his music-world, knew nothing of human life.

'Will you play to me ?' he said, after a pause. ' I long to hear Melusina again.'

As he leaned back listening, he wondered whether the passion of that wonderful music was real or fictitious; then whether the world of imagination or the material world was the most real, the most actual. The lovely harmony affected him powerfully ; but through it all the thought of bright little gay Assunta lying white and dead, with her little baby on her cold breast, brought the tears to his eyes.

CHAPTER IV.

SIR EUSTACE persuaded Ursel to spend Sunday with him. Lady Bellingham had never cared for her son's friend, but she could not complain of his presence, for it was the first circumstance that brought back one ray of interest or pleasure to his life. It broke through the deadly monotony of the days at Castleford, which was beginning to tell on her also. For a time she had solaced her- self with the home-truths to which Georgie had alluded. There was a kind of finite force about them that was agreeable and sustaining to her ; but, unfortunately, they seemed somewhat to have lost their power to sting. Her son was too listless to heed the constant repetition of the wholesome ' I told you so,' and of late Lady Bellingham had ended her little homilies with a weary yawn. Her brother, at least, was a more satisfactory victim. The worthy Rector was overwhelmed with remorse at the part that he himself had played in the tragedy, and it was a real source of comfort to Lady Bellingham that she had him to torment. They wondered how it would all end, when Eustace would rouse himself and go away, or take any kind of step. There was nothing for it but patience. Eustace himself knew neither what to do nor whither to go, or, indeed, whether it would be best to go or stay. He was utterly miserable ; he had upon him a crushing sense of failure in every undertaking in life. His old regiment was abroad on active duty. He would have given the world to have been with them had he still had that duty to fulfil; but he felt that he could not, and ought not, to leave England. Sometimes he shrank from moving, at others he loathed every road, every wall, every tree of his beloved old home, feeling as if they asked him what he had done with the little tender young wife to whom he owed so much.

He and Ursel wandered together all through the woods. To the musician they seemed a very fairyland of beauty, and his naïve admiration pleased his host. They passed through the same paths in which Eustace had first met Kitty, and walked with her through the lights and shadows, listening to the gentle voice which his heart so ached to hear once more. He remembered her quiet words, her sympathy, the little set phrases in which she expressed

44—2

herself: they all came home to him so vividly that he could not suppress a sigh so bitter that it was almost a groan.

Ursel looked at him with compassion.

'Let us sit down,' he said. 'You English do not put your sad thoughts into words, and I also am like an Englishman in that; but there are times when it is well to break through this cold reserve. Life is short; one does not want one's heart to break.'

'Tell me about yourself,' said Eustace, throwing himself on the turf. 'That is far more interesting to me than anything relative to my own affairs.'

'A man who has in his life one great and absorbing thought, as I have,' said Ursel thoughtfully, 'cannot understand quite why you others make so much of domestic life. To you, it is all in all; to us, it is but the background of the picture.'

'Is it so?' said Eustace. 'Then to you your music is the actual reality—not the representation or interpretation of reality?'

'Ah! there we musicians are different from you. Of course it is reality. You figure to yourselves a thousand interpretations of the music to which you listen—fictitious fancies; but one thing is actual—the music which has no interpretation, for it is an ego of its own. The great composers saw no visions of love or beauty or the forces of Nature in their works : they were absorbed in a higher culte than human nature offered them, and that culte is Harmony.'

'Then you hold yourselves above the joys and woes of common men?'

Ursel paused a moment, and then said deliberately :

'Yes; were it otherwise, we should not be great.'

'Ambition *versus* happiness.'

'You put it so. Well, I accept it. Happiness! why, happiness is not worth a thought. Who would not sacrifice it to ambition, to success, to work, to unknown possibilities? There is but one perfect satisfaction of ourselves on earth.'

'And that is——'

'To be Lord Mayor of London.'

'My dear Ursel!'

'It is so. The highest ambition of the aspirant attained, he can mount no higher. It lasts a year, he is saved from satiety, and he possesses for his ripe old age the glorious memory of what has been. Do not laugh.'

'Ah! do you remember telling me that you were not ambitious?'

'Did I so? The day was when applause was nothing to me.'

'And now?'

'I could not live without it,' he said, low and eagerly.

'Tell me,' said Eustace, 'did this ambition of yours wake up when your wife died?'

'No, no; before that. I do not think,' he went on slowly, 'that Assunta's death had any very great or marked effect upon my life; as I said before, to men like myself domestic bliss is not the prominent thought of life. I grieved for her. Do not mistake me.'

'Ah! but Ursel, forgive me, did you ever know love—what I call love? Assunta was very sweet and young and gay, but——'

'She is dead!' said Ursel softly; and his friend felt that he could say no more.

There was a pause, then Ursel spoke suddenly and vehemently:

'We talk of ambition, but it is difficult

for a man to rise who is fettered as I am—bound hand and foot. I am not my own master; my very art is the property of another man. It is hard to suffer for the ignorance of one's youth!'

'Can nothing be done? Could you not pay off this *impresario?*'

'Pay him off! by borrowing the money on my prospects at a high rate of interest—that is, by exchanging one master for another.'

'We will talk it over together, and consult Mulroy. You would not object, Ursel?'

'Object? No, no! You have been too good a friend to me for that. Ah!' cried the musician, throwing wide his arms. 'If I could be free, I should indeed be a happy man!'

'The same good fairy who sent you Melusina might come forward once more.'

'Ah, who knows?' Ursel laughed glee-fully. 'Melusina and I might rule the music world if we were but free. Do you remember your telling me that no man knew himself until he had succeeded?'

'Yes,' answered Eustace. 'And you answered me that no man knew himself until he had failed.'

'Failure, failure!' cried Ursel. 'That is a bitter word.'

'So bitter,' answered Eustace, 'that you may pray to God, night and day, to send you any form of trial rather than that; for it saps the very root of life, and, by destroying self-confidence, diminishes all future possibilities.'

'My poor friend!'

'Then it is settled,' said Eustace abruptly. 'I shall go up to London with you to-morrow. We will consult Mulroy, and see my lawyer, and consider what can be done.'

' You will come with me ?'

' I will.'

' I am glad indeed.'

Great was Lady Bellingham's astonishment when she heard that Eustace was going away the next day. She found it necessary to blame his doing so ; but in her heart of hearts she was overjoyed. She could not have endured her present life much longer.

Sir Eustace departed, full of interest in the object of his journey. But, strange to say, a sense of disappointment had come over him in his intercourse with Ursel. In former days he had felt that he exercised an extraordinary influence over him ; but now this influence seemed to have vanished —to be merged into admiration for the great musician, for the rising man. Ursel was no longer the strangely sympathetic, thoughtful man he had known and loved. His thoughts and mind and soul were now so wrapped up in his art and its success that he dwelt in a separate world. The great maelström of triumph had seized him in its dizzy grasp. The old self was gone for ever.

CHAPTER V.

EUSTACE and Ursel parted at the railway-station; the former to go to his own house in Eaton Square, the latter to return to his many engagements.

The rooms of his London house were to Eustace haunted by remembrances of his young wife. How gaily they had furnished them together! How bright and sweet and sunshiny she had been for a short time at the beginning of their married life, before the blight of disappointment had begun to wither the hope in her breast! Looking back at those days, he found it difficult to analyze his own feelings. He had been very fond of her then. It might have ripened into warmer feeling but for the strong, though unexpressed, opinion which shone through every word and action of his favourite sister, that he was bound to be faithful to the memory of past days.

He now realized that women dwell on trifles in a way that men little dream of. A careless word, a little slighting action, which are forgotten by them as soon as done or uttered, live in the woman's heart and give her pain years after she has forgiven, but has never forgotten. And so a mere look, a quick caress, a tender word, will often, as the long dark years roll onward, be more glowing landmarks in their memory than tangible events to a man.

Kitty's landmarks were all of this character. Their importance in her life was very disproportionate to what they were in his.

Alice Bellingham came to her brother's house with trembling hands and a beating heart. She longed, yet dreaded beyond measure, to have an explanation with him. He would far rather have escaped it, have let things drift on until time had softened his feeling towards her ; but she could not bear it in her impatient misery.

He was not at home when she went, so she sat down in his room and determined to wait there until he came in.

Eustace was very busy all the afternoon. He went to see the agents who had conducted the search for his lost young wife. He steeled himself to go through all their long weary particulars as to what had been done and what remained to do ; and he gave them fresh orders, feeling all the time that it was not in this way that she would be found.

He saw his lawyer, and talked over Ursel's bond with his *impresario;* and it was settled that he should thoroughly go into the business with Ursel. Then he went to his club, and dined there, meeting several friends, so that it was nearly eleven o'clock before he returned home.

Alice was wearied out; she lay back in a great armchair in his room, and from her fatigue she had fallen so fast asleep that she did not move when he came in.

Eustace came and stood beside her, looking down on her. In the calm of sleep she looked so wearied out, so sad, so pretty, that a tender feeling of compassion came over him; he bent down and kissed her. The kiss awakened her, and she sprang up frightened; but when she saw him looking at her with that tender, pitying look in the eyes that had grown so terribly sad, she put out her arms and drew him towards her, bursting into a passion of tears as she sobbed :

'Eustace, Eustace, only forgive me! Only say you forgive me!'

He put his arm round her.

'We have both need of forgiveness,' he said. 'How can I blame you, Alice, when I am a thousand times more to blame than you are?'

'Oh, believe me, Eustace, there is nothing in the wide world I would not do to bring her back!'

'I do believe you,' he said earnestly. Her excessive emotion frightened him. 'And, Alice, some day, if we can only find her, I shall be able to convince her—all may yet be well.'

Alice could not hope; she had seen Kitty's face. It seemed to her that, as he had not seen that, he could not know what the blow had been.

'I don't know what to say to you,' she said in bitter tears. 'I did not mean to be unkind. I thought I was your best and only friend—the only one who cared for May. I meant to be so kind. I was blind, blind, and it was all cruelty instead.'

He stroked her hand gently; he also was feeling this. He could not contradict her.

'I only thought of you—only of you, my own brother. I never thought of her.'

'Ah! there lay the terrible mistake,' he said. 'You forgot that she was my wife; harm to her was harm to me. But do not cry like that, Alice; perhaps you exaggerate. Kitty always seemed to me to be so fond of you.'

'Oh! perhaps that is the worst reproach of all. She was fond of me; she looked to me to help her, and I failed her. Oh, Eustace, how I failed her!'

'Poor Alice!'

'You may indeed pity me! How shall I ever forgive myself? I might have done so much, and I let her drift on, growing every day more sad and more dispirited; and this is the end.'

Eustace did not answer. How bitterly he was feeling it, he alone knew.

'Poor Kitty! poor little gentle thing! but indeed, indeed, I never thought of injury to her. I only thought of you. Oh, Eustace! you may forgive me, and Kitty would, I know, a thousand times over, but I never, never can forgive myself.'

'Alice,' said her brother hoarsely, 'can you suggest nothing? Have you no idea of where she can be gone?'

Alice shook her head. 'I fancied that she might have gone to St. Cuthbert's, where

May works so much ; and I went there and saw Sister Harriet, but she was not there. It was only a vague idea.'

' You think she will come back ?'

'No; she will never come back,' cried Alice.

' Do not say that !' he exclaimed, almost roughly. ' Do not doom me to a lifelong remorse. Kitty is good as a saint. There is the marriage vow ; she will not break it—she cannot.'

' If you were dying, or in great need, she would come back,' said Alice.

Eustace did not answer ; the pain was too great.

Alice presently rose to her feet, and pushed back her hair.

' Eustace,' she said, ' thank you for being like your own self to me again. If you can, will you let me help you ? You know there is nothing that I would not do.'

He kissed her.

'Help me,' he said. 'My poor Alice, I have need of help. Between us all, we must find her.'

'Yes,' said Alice, trying to speak brightly; 'we must find her.'

The night was fine, and very warm. Eustace asked her whether she would not walk home to the Mulroys' house, and they started together. The streets and squares were very silent, but now and then they passed a house where entertainment was going on. Carriages rattled past them— linkmen shouted.

Alice clung closely to her brother's arm. It was so sweet to be at peace with him again. Her eyes were full of soft tears; her aching heart was lulled and soothed by this forgiveness and reunion, and she felt braced up to hope again.

They went on together, speaking little, both absorbed in thought.

Passing through Belgrave Square, at the door of a quiet house stood a single brougham. There had been one, or at most two, guests in that house that night.

They were about to pass, when the door was thrown open, and the guests came out. Eustace for one moment stood still, and a sharp shudder went through him.

How beautiful she was, and how un-changed! She passed close to him, leaning on her husband's arm. He saw the stately movement he knew so well; he saw the gleam of diamonds on the white hand that for one second rested on the door, and heard her speak :

' Do you walk home, Austen ?'

Only that—only one glance of violet eyes waiting for the answer ; but in the glance, in the tone, was some subtle magic that told him, as clearly as if it had been uttered in plain words, that Marion loved her husband.

The brougham drove away. Lord Austen stood for one moment on the doorstep, lighting his cigar ; then he looked up and perceived Eustace and his sister.

'Is it you, my dear, dear Bellingham?' he exclaimed. 'Is it really you and Alice? I did not know you were in London. How are you? Where are you staying?'

He spoke with volubility, anxious to hide how the change in his friend's looks horrified him.

'You have come back?' said Eustace, moistening his dry lips. 'I thought that, like other people, you would have gone abroad.'

'We are going abroad when the weather is a little cooler,' answered Lord Austen. 'We have been dining with my old aunt.

We are only passing through London. And you?'

'I don't know,' answered Eustace. 'I have no plans.'

'Will you tell Marion that I will come and see her to-morrow?' said Alice, steadying her voice. 'Are you in Brook Street?'

'Yes, just for a few days. Do come and see her. Let me walk home with you,' he went on, in his eager kindness.

Eustace would gladly have refused, but he could not. He was grateful to Lord Austen for going on talking without ceasing till they reached the Mulroys' house.

Alice went in. It was twelve o'clock. Georgie had gone to bed, but Joe was up. He asked no questions, only was very gentle and attentive to her, making her eat the soup and sandwiches that were waiting for her. She had never felt so softened or so kindly towards him, and her 'Good-night' was warmer than it ever had been before.

Meanwhile, Lord Austen had passed his arm through that of Eustace, and led him away.

'Come in here, old fellow,' he said, taking from his pocket the key of the square, which he had asked for at the Mulroys' house. 'It is an odd place of resort at this time of night, but it will do as well as anything else. I want to talk to you.'

It was dark in the square; as the two men paced up and down, the ends of their cigars made two red sparks in the darkness.

'You are terribly down, Eu,' said Lord Austen; 'I can see it in your face, old man. If I could be of the smallest use to you——'

'I do not see how you can,' said Eustace

hoarsely. 'Forgive me, but there are some things one cannot speak of.'

'I know, I know; I would not intrude for the world. But——'

He paused, and cleared his throat.

'We are in an odd position with regard to each other, Eustace.'

'That is it,' said Eustace, almost fiercely. 'Take care what you say.'

'There are times in which it is best to speak quite plainly,' said Lord Austen; 'and I will ask you to bear with me, for a good reason. I cannot but think it possible that I—that we may hear of your wife before you do.'

Eustace started violently.

'Why should you say so?' he exclaimed.

'I will tell you why. A short time ago, on the very day before her father died, Lady Bellingham had a long conversation with May.'

'You cannot mean it? When and where did they meet?'

'We met at Marshall and Snelgrove's, and they went back to Mr. Austen's house together. May told me about the interview afterwards.'

'I did not know that they knew each other.'

'The acquaintance was very slight, but Lady Bellingham (forgive me if I must pain you) seemed to cling to May so much.'

'It is very strange,' said Eustace thoughtfully. 'Never mind pain or any such humbug; only tell me all you can.'

'I have not much to tell,' said Lord Austen; 'and if you would rather hear it from May herself——'

Eustace shook his head with a slight, rapid movement. Lord Austen went on:

'Well, your wife seemed very far from happy. She poured it all out to May.'

'Was there any especial cause?' asked Eustace.

'Not that I can make out. It was not any one thing that had happened more or less. She was overwrought, worn out, poor little thing! She loved you so entirely, she said, and was so full of remorse and self-distrust because she had got into her head (as women will do sometimes) that—that——'

'That I did not care for her. Do not spare me, Austen,' said Eustace bitterly.

'I think it was not only that,' said Lord Austen gently. 'She never blamed you, poor little gentle heart! Her remorse was for her own part. She thought that she had done you harm (forgive me, Eustace); your life had grown hard and bitter.'

Eustace cleared his throat.

'What did Marion say?' he asked.

'May could only soothe and comfort her,

and most earnestly, most beseechingly en-
treated her to persevere and try to win her
right place in your heart.'

'Had she then thought of leaving
me?'

The hoarse, changed voice of his friend
was so painful that Lord Austen could
hardly persevere.

'Not in that way, Eustace. I only tell
you this because both May and I fancy that,
with her wonderfully loving, tender nature,
she will pine for news of you, and we
think she will come or communicate with
May.'

'And on this state of mind fell Alice's
cruel words.'

Eustace was speaking to himself. He
walked on silently for a moment. Then he
said :

' Austen, when she comes, what will you
—what will May say to her?'

'What may we say? Do you not see that is what I want to know?'

Eustace turned round, speaking passionately:

'What can I say? Let me put it to yourself, Austen. Does such love as yours and mine has been ever come twice in a life? It is a strange thing to say to you. Answer me as frankly as I ask it of you.'

Lord Austen paused for a moment; then he looked up and laid his hand on his friend's shoulder.

'Men say that it does, Eu. I cannot say. Do you remember the cry of Esau? "Hast thou but one blessing, O my father?"'

'It is an anomaly for Jacob to comfort Esau,' said Eustace, with a low, bitter laugh. 'An incongruity—eh, Austen?'

Lord Austen did not answer for a moment.

What could he say? It seemed as if only now that he had gained the peerless woman for his wife whom he had wooed so long, could he understand the utter blank and loss to his friend.

'I am the last man in the world who should venture to preach to you,' he said at last. 'But this I will tell you frankly. Years ago I would have resigned every hope, every joy of my life, could I have made you and Marion happy; but it was not possible. . . . Only believe me when I tell you this, for it is true; and in that time in which I suffered the same suffering that you also have known, I learnt one lesson: there is something higher even than love, and that is duty.'

'Cold comfort for the wife,' said Eustace. 'My conscience acquits me there. I did my duty.'

Lord Austen said nothing for a moment.

He passed his hand through his hair, and sighed. It seemed a hopeless, terrible entanglement.

'Why did you marry her?' he exclaimed suddenly.

Eustace started.

'There are few men who would venture to ask me such a question,' he said haughtily.

'I would not have done so,' said Lord Austen, his face flushing, 'were I not convinced, of course, that the motive was not a mercenary one. But why did you do it?'

'Reasons are complicated. This is a moment of strictest confidence. My mother told me—well, I had better tell the truth—that my poor Kitty cared for me. I was very unhappy, and——'

'I understand. But surely Lady Belling-ham does not know?'

'Unfortunately she overheard some words the women were saying—a number of them together—and this was the end of it.'

'Poor little thing, poor little gentle soul!'

'What can I do?'

'I am afraid it is a matter of patience. I still adhere to my belief that she will come to May. But if she does come—that is what grieves me so—what can we say to her?'

'Tell her she has become necessary to me. Tell her that I cannot live without her!' exclaimed Eustace passionately.

'I may tell her that?'

'But she will not come!' His tone once more became dejected. 'It is no use to deceive one's self—she will not come. She will never forgive me!'

'Patience and courage,' said Lord Austen hopefully. 'Now, Eustace, it is very late; shall we go home?'

They went as far as their roads lay together, then stopped to say good-night.

'Eustace, only one more word. Will you, would you, come and see May?'

He shook his head — no other answer would come —, and walked off down the street.

CHAPTER VI.

WHEN Kitty Bellingham left Castleford there was but one feeling in her breast—one passionate longing to set her husband free ; to hide herself out of his way ; to sever herself from him altogether.

Alice's words, acting on a nature already too much inclined, both by nature and education, to a morbid distrust of self, had for the moment almost overturned her reason. It seemed to her that she must have acted with want of reserve, have betrayed her feelings with a shameless want of modesty and reticence, or it never could have happened. To so sensitive a woman the sense of shame was intolerable.

As she sat in the train on her solitary journey up to London, the torrent of blood kept rushing up into her cheeks, making them burn with painful blushes, making her temples throb and her breathing quick from this new kind of misery.

What must he have thought of her? What a contempt he must have felt for her! Poor Kitty did not know how to bear it. And they all knew it—those women who belonged to him ; her own mother knew it, and had allowed her to do it. She felt as if she had nowhere to turn, no refuge in all the world.

When she arrived at Euston Square, and found herself alone in London, she experienced, at first, an overpowering sense of bewilderment ; but no one would have imagined it who saw her quiet movements and self-possessed manner. She went into the refreshment-room and asked for a glass of water, and she sat down on a horse-hair sofa to drink it and decide what she should do next.

People came in and out, but nobody noticed her; and she had time to think. Her first impulse was to go to Marion Austen—to fly to that strong, loving nature which had revealed to her some of its strength and beauty so short a time ago. Then it flashed across her the recollection of what had happened; of the commencement of this terrible catastrophe. Marion was married—she was Lord Austen's wife. Kitty clenched her teeth tightly to keep back the little moans which came to her lips as she thought of what this news would have been to her if her husband had loved her only a very little.

She could not go to Marion ; she could not introduce her own unhappiness on the mingled sorrow and bliss of that bride. And a strange contradictory feeling sprang up in her breast—a jealousy for Eustace that May should have forgotten him at last. Poor Kitty! The tide of conflicting feelings was utterly exhausting.

She rose at last, carrying the travelling-bag which held money and that knitting that used so to worry her husband. She walked away from the station for some way, then she hailed a cab and drove to Waterloo Station. She took a ticket and went down to Dover.

Kitty could not have told why she went there; but it suited her well. People looked a little strangely at her when they found that she had no luggage, but they agreed that it was no affair of theirs at the hotel.

Every day Kitty went down to the shore,

and stood or sat there for hours watching the great waves come tumbling in. Her mind was always dwelling on the one point —the sense of humiliation which over-powered her. There was danger for Kitty at that time, danger from the frightful force of the concentration of thought. It was apparently visible to outsiders.

Among the visitors at Dover just then was an old lady whose seventy-six years of life had been spent in going about doing good; one of those people who through their long pilgrimage have gathered deep experience, and to whom human suffering lies open as in a book which they alone can read.

Old Mrs. Huntingford used to watch Kitty on the sands, and she saw well that there was something terribly wrong. The white fixed lips, the strained blue eyes, the little twitch of eyelid and throat—nothing escaped her notice. She had daughters of her own : one married in India, out of sight but ever in her heart ; one closer still—in Paradise.

Kitty was standing watching the waves when she felt a gentle hand laid on her shoulder, and turning round she saw that sweet aged face looking into hers.

'Are you not well, dear?' she said gently.

She was only just in time.

Kitty put both hands to her throat where the agonizing neuralgia was throbbing; then she uttered a kind of cry, and would have fallen had not the kind Samaritan caught her in her arms and called her maid to help her.

Mrs. Huntingford had the poor little insensible form carried into her own house, which was close by; and she sent for a doctor, and engaged a nurse, and prepared to nurse her through the fluctuating stages of an illness which but narrowly escaped brain-fever.

Again and again the faithful maid warned her mistress, and pointed out all sorts of strange incongruities. The poor young patient had no luggage but a few necessaries bought in haste, yet her clothes were costly, and she wore splendid rings. But the worst of it all was the way that in her wanderings she was always babbling of shame—nothing but shame, and what should she do, and whither go.

Mrs. Huntingford used to look very grave when she came from her bedside, and very anxious; but she would think no ill of her.

'There are many kinds of shame, my dear Parsons,' she said, when her maid was remonstrating one day. 'Some kinds of shame are so beneficial that I wish you had a touch of it ; for shame, to think evil of a creature you know nothing about !'

Parsons was as kind-hearted as she was prudent.

' I will do my best for her, whatever she may be,' she said ; ' but don't say that I did not warn you, ma'am.'

' No, I won't say so,' said her mistress, smiling. ' You shall have your due.'

At last one evening when the setting sun was going down redly into the sea, and the glare of its light was shining into her room, Kitty opened her eyes with the light of intelligence once more in their gaze. Mrs. Huntingford was sitting by her, and caught the first word that she uttered.

' Mamma !'

There was something homely, simple, and comfortable in that, which reassured her friend on the spot. She spoke as if to her own daughter.

'Your mamma has not come yet, my child; meanwhile, take this and try to go to sleep.'

Kitty was too weak to ask questions; she felt a gentle motherly hand on her brow. She drank the soup offered her, and from that time began to sleep herself into convalescence.

A week or two passed; at last a time came when the doctor decreed that she might be questioned. He did not quite like the perfectly quiescent apathetic condition into which she appeared to be sinking; he thought that, even at the risk of some harm from over-excitement, it might be well to find out something about her relations.

Mrs. Huntingford began it.

Kitty had been moved to a sofa and placed in a bay-window overlooking the sea; the windows were wide open; the even plash of the waves fell with a dull, soft monotony on the sands.

Mrs. Huntingford was embroidering one of the most elaborate patterns of modern art. She began to ask questions in a matter - of - fact way, without looking at Kitty.

'Where is your husband now, my dear?' she said.

'At Castleford,' she answered. 'They were all there.'

Then Kitty stopped suddenly, and the colour rushed into her face.

'He must be getting very anxious about you,' went on Mrs. Huntingford. 'Don't you think we ought to write to him, or to your mamma?'

'Oh no—no!'

'But they cannot know where you are?'

'Do you think I am likely to die?' said

Kitty very suddenly. 'Is that why you want to write?'

'No, dear child; you are not in the least likely to die, thank God!'

'Ah!'

There was such profound dejection in that little exclamation that her friend looked at her, and said tenderly:

'Will you not tell me all about it, my poor child? Would it not do you good?'

Kitty put out her arms, and held up her face to be kissed.

'Not to-day,' she said very sadly; 'I cannot to-day!'

Mrs. Huntingford was content to wait for a few days, and Kitty grew strong rapidly. She was soon able to go out for some hours at a time, and lie upon the sands; and she began to eat more, and to have a bright, tender, pink colour in her cheeks.

'To-morrow, to-morrow, you shall know all about it,' she said one night, as her old friend bent over her to give her a last kiss in her bed. 'I am not at all mysterious, and my story is very simple. Some day mamma and I will both thank you ; no words can ever express my gratitude for all you have been to me, but God will reward you, dearest, dearest Mrs. Huntingford !'

'And some day you and your husband will come and stay with me, and tell me all about the foolish quarrel that I think you must have had. There, that is my theory about you.'

Poor Kitty's lips were quivering.

'My dear,' said the old lady earnestly, 'did you ever read Tennyson's exquisite poem called " The First Quarrel"? '

She shook her head.

'Well, be still and listen to me. In that short poem lies one of the most complete tragedies of human life. There was a young wife ; she was angry with her husband—justly angry, mind you—and she spoke bitter words, and he was going to sea. She let him go unforgiven, with the angry words ringing in his ears, and her passionate reproaches in his heart. The last words of the poem comprise the anguish of a lifetime :

> ' " An' the boat went down that night,
> The boat went down that night." '

Kitty hid her face and trembled.

' Poor little thing !' said Mrs. Huntingford. ' I will not tease you any more to-night ; only remember, child, that there may come a day in which the words " Too late " are an agony too great for human endurance.'

Mrs. Huntingford went away, and Kitty lay for many hours wide awake, listening to the waves. She was not thinking of what she would do, or where she would go ; it seemed as if her head were too tired to form plans—as if she must wait, as she had waited before, for the inspiration of the moment.

The next morning she slept very late, and only rose about twelve o'clock, feeling with a kind of terror that her rest was over, that to-day she must give the long-promised explanations.

Kitty went out on the beach presently with her books and a shawl, and she sat down in a favourite sheltered corner watching the sea. Mrs. Huntingford settled her comfortably there, and then left her and went indoors ; she had letters to write, and could not spare the morning.

Then Kitty rose up quietly, and walked away into the town ; a sort of feeling had again come irresistibly upon her that she must disappear again. She hardly knew what she dreaded ; she fancied that all these good and kind friends would combine and force her to go back to Eustace, and this she could not bear—to be again forced upon him, again made to appeal to his compassion.

If she had thought it all out previously, she could not have devised a better plan ; but she had arranged nothing—only a kind of instinct guided her, as an instinct guides the hunted hare, teaching it to double on its pursuers.

Kitty went to the station. She had still plenty of money. She took a ticket for London, and started. She did not go far on her journey. She got out at the first station, took a carriage, and drove to Folkestone Pier. The boat was just starting, and no one noticed her as she went quietly on board. In two hours she was in France.

Mrs. Huntingford did everything that lay in her power. During the last fortnight, unknown to Kitty, she had sent an advertisement to several papers, carefully worded, but containing a description sufficiently accurate to attract attention, and giving her own address.

That very afternoon, excited by the wording of the advertisement, Sir Eustace Bellingham arrived at Dover. He found Mrs. Huntingford in great trouble. Her description made him recognise his wife beyond a doubt. The disappointment was terrible. He telegraphed for a detective, and the search began again. The ticket taken to London appeared conclusive ; and every gentle-looking woman in a black gown who had travelled up to London that day was traced elaborately to her own destination and identification ; but all in vain.

Kitty had once more succeeded in baffling pursuit.

CHAPTER VII.

EUSTACE came into the Mulroys' dining-room. They were just finishing dinner. Georgie could hardly suppress the sorrowful exclamation that rose to her lips when she saw her brother; he looked so haggard, so worn-out and discouraged.

They were alone, Alice the only guest, and they hastily dismissed the servants.

'No news, Eustace?' said Alice eagerly. 'I am afraid you have nothing good to tell us.'

'I was too late,' he answered.

Mr. Mulroy poured out a glass of wine and pushed it towards him.

'Then it was Kitty?'

'Yes, it must have been Kitty ; it could have been nobody else. She had been very ill, and that good Mrs. Huntingford nursed her through it all, knowing nothing about her in any way. That woman is kindness and sweetness itself. One does not know how to thank her.'

'But how can you be sure that it was Kitty ?'

'It must have been ; everything answers to it. And in her wandering she was always speaking of her mother and of me. And, besides, they had cut off long locks of her hair. In short, it was indubitable.'

'But, Eustace, where is she ?'

'The very morning that I went there she had gone away, had left no message, no letter, nothing to identify her. She had apparently gone up to London. She was recognised at the station, but there it ended. We have not been able to trace her farther.'

Alice sighed deeply, and tried to brush away the tears of disappointment unseen.

Joe Mulroy bent forward.

'Keep up heart, Eustace,' he said. 'You know this kind of thing cannot go on. When she wants money she must send to the bank. We must find her some day.'

There was nothing more to say. They went upstairs to the drawing-room, and tried to talk of other things.

'How much longer do you mean to stay in London?' Eustace asked.

Georgie looked doubtful.

'I don't know what to say,' she said. 'We are anxious to get down to the Isle of Wight, but while there is anything to keep us waiting——'

'There is nothing to wait for,' he answered quickly, almost impatiently. 'London is intolerable. If you will let me, I will come with you.'

'Oh, Eustace! will you really?' exclaimed Georgie; and Alice looked up, hardly believing so good a piece of news.

'Yes,' he said. 'Have you room on the yacht, or is your party made up?'

'We have no party,' said Joe eagerly. 'I put them all off long ago, as our plans were so uncertain. It will, indeed, be quite delightful to have you.'

'Where shall we go?'

'To the Mediterranean; don't you think so? Let us try and see something new.'

Alice went for an atlas, and they were bending over it, when a servant came in to ask whether Mr. Mulroy would see Monsieur Ursel for a moment.

In answer to their consent they heard a

quick step come up the stairs, and in one moment Ursel came in. He was in evening dress, and had evidently but a few moments to spare.

There was something extraordinary in his face, so extraordinary that Joe Mulroy and Eustace glanced at each other.

'I suppose the look of intoxication from excess of happiness is so rare on a human face that it frightens one,' Joe said afterwards to his wife.

It was excitement, ecstasy, that lighted it up—his eyes shone, his cheeks burned, the smile played round his mouth. He came into the room with outstretched hands.

'My friends, my friends!' he cried; 'have you heard it? Do you know? I am free!'

They gathered round him.

'You have heard from Mr. Calloway?' they asked.

'Heard ? Have I not heard, indeed ? Great news ! Glorious news ! News to make a man mad or drunk with joy ! What have I done to deserve such happiness ?'

'Sit down, Ursel,' said Eustace, putting his hand on his shoulder. The frightful excitement of the musician startled him. 'Sit down, and tell us all about it.'

'I have only ten minutes,' said Ursel ; 'I am at St. James's Hall. I have played once already. I shall be wanted again at ten. You see, I must not delay. You ask for details ; what can I say ? I have only received a notification from Mr. Calloway, your agent, to say that the money has been paid, and that I am a free man.'

'But who paid it ? How did you raise it ?'

'Who ? Ah ! some day — some day, perhaps, when life is over, and we meet in the other world, the angels will point him out to me, but not now.'

'You do not know?'

'It is the same hand that sent me Melusina—the warm heart, the golden soul for whom night and day I pray as I never yet have prayed for father or mother, wife or child.'

This violent excitement had a strange effect on the listeners—it almost shocked them.

'Is the matter concluded?' said Eustace, trying, by speaking in a commonplace voice, to draw back Ursel into calmer regions.

'Did you not hear? It is done, com_ pleted, paid over ; and such a sum ! Good heavens, what a sum ! Who can have done it ? Who can have had the greatness of soul ; who could have had the passion for music that would rise to such a height as this? See, I have the receipt, the actual receipt!'

He tried one pocket after another ; as he did so the colour dying out of his face, leaving it livid.

'Not there!' he exclaimed. Then, with almost a shout: 'Am I, then, mad—delirious? Is it a dream? Ah!'

The colour rushed back with such violence as almost to cause a convulsion. He had found the paper. The room reeled before his eyes. He steadied himself by the table, trying to see through the red mist before him.

Eustace laid his hand on his shoulder. The kindly voice sounded miles off in the rushing sound in his ears.

'Come, come, Ursel—steady! It is all right ; you have it in your hand.'

They made him sit down, and Joe Mulroy brought him a glass of water, and un-

loosened the collar, which seemed to suffo-
cate him. It passed off as quickly as it had
come on, and Ursel seemed unconscious of
what had happened.

'Now then, you are yourself again,' said
Sir Eustace quietly. 'Come downstairs
and have a cigar, and get steady, or you will
never be ready to play again by ten
o'clock.'

'What o'clock is it now?' said Ursel, with
a violent start.

'Not past nine yet. Steady, old fellow!'
said Eustace. He took his arm, and led
him from the room downstairs.

'What a frightful thing it will be if that
man ever fails!' said Alice, with a slight
shudder. 'There was something about him
to-night that frightened me.'

'How curiously changed he is!' said
Georgie. 'If I had been asked to describe
him as we used to know him, I should have

said that he was one of the quietest, most unambitious, philosophical characters I ever met.'

'I wonder whether we all have hidden in us such violent passions,' said Alice ; 'and that if anything came to awaken them, like this man's marvellous success, whether we also should lose our self-control.'

'I hope not,' said Georgie. 'If I saw you like that, I should treat it for hysterics.'

Alice laughed, and then sighed.

'Poor Ursel !' she said. 'How little we knew him, and how little he knew himself in old days !'

'I suppose the poor little silly wife, with her prosy interpretations of his music, and her incessant chatter about her neighbours and their new gowns and bonnets, was an excellent balance for him.'

'Yet one pitied him for the incongruity.'

'I think, on the whole, sometimes, Providence knows best.'

Alice laughed again.

'Well, perhaps,' she said.   'Certainly there must be a strange want of discipline in his character.'

Downstairs, Ursel wanted to pace up and down the room, but his two friends would not allow it.   They sent for iced lemonade; they plied him with cigars.   The first two went out almost directly; the third asserted its calming influence.   Ursel ceased to talk feverishly.   He leant back in his chair.   He began to examine his hands attentively.

Neither of the Englishmen had spoken for some time.   They also were smoking. Then Eustace said quietly:

'What is the matter with your hands, Ursel?   Are you not used to the sight of them?'

'Matter?—nothing.   I always take great

care of my hands; they are my fortune, you see. They are all right. Just now they were sometimes cold, sometimes hot, and inclined to shake. Now the fingers have recovered themselves. They are strong as iron, and soft too.'

Eustace took one of his long, shapely hands into his own, and looked at it curiously. It was a nervous hand that night; pulses beating, and inclined to quiver. He laid it down as if it had been some delicate musical instrument.

'I suppose we ought to go,' he said, glancing at his watch.

Joe Mulroy rang the bell.

'I think I shall go to St. James's Hall for half an hour,' he said. 'What do you say, Eustace—shall we?'

'With all my heart.'

Ursel thought places might be found, and they started.

The hall was crowded; there was not a single vacant seat. Ursel's fame had risen to the highest pitch known in London. The brothers-in-law did not mind standing ; they found just sufficient room for that.

When Ursel came on he was perfectly calm—almost dreamy. What had passed seemed to fade into unreality. As usual, he was not quite satisfied with one string of Melusina—he tried it again and again. It was strange ; everyone was convinced of its perfection of tune but himself. He tried the patience of his great audience. It had an odd effect on Eustace, the twanging of that particular note. It carried him back to old days; to the little yellow-washed salon, the small music-world of Santa Chiara, the calm and quiet and repose of the musician's life there. Why was Ursel so long over it ? Was it that there was one note always acting as a subtle jar on

his over-strained nerves? It ended at last,
and he began to play. It was a great
triumph, a magnificent success ; but the
ever-recurring encores and apparently endless applause did not bring back to Ursel's
face the wild look of excitement that had
startled them so much in Eaton Square.
He bowed very calmly with his old dignity.
When his friends sought him after the con-
cert was over, they heard that he had gone
without waiting to bid them good-night.

CHAPTER VIII.

THE heat at Santa Chiara that summer was very unusual even for Italy. Day after day the sky was perfectly cloudless ; the fiery sun poured down relentlessly on town and country; the nights were hot and airless as the days. No sweet, cool evening breeze came to freshen the heavy atmosphere; the oppression was very great.

Trade languished. Nobody went out into the streets unless they could help it ; the pavement seemed to blister their feet.

Don Paolo and his mother never left

Santa Chiara. Long ago she had settled there. It was the home of her married life, the scene of her husband's death, and she had never left it since. She belonged to the Dominican Order without vows, and her life was often much like that of a Sister of Charity, with a combination of intercourse with a few friends and a considerable love of society. Madame di St. Isidoro was not naturally fond of good works, but the influence of her son and the constant sight of his devoted and self-sacrificing life had aroused within her the longing to work for God.

There was sickness in Santa Chiara, low fever lingering in the town, a general listlessness and want of energy.

Don Paolo came into his mother's rooms one day with anxiety in his face. She no longer inhabited the upstairs rooms, but had moved into the large cool salons that the Bellinghams had occupied. The sun was closely shut out from them, and the doors replaced by curtains. They were, comparatively, wonderfully cool.

Don Paolo sat down and passed his hands through his hair.

'Bad news, madamina,' he said. 'I have bad news to give you.'

'More bad news? Come, Paolo, courage! What is it?'

'The fountain has failed—the Bruzzi fountain. No water flows. They have reached the bottom. There is nothing but mud, and mud of an evil smell.'

'That is bad,' said Marie thoughtfully. 'What is there to depend on now?'

The Priore shrugged his shoulders.

'We must economize water, madamina,' he said. 'For instance——'

He made a slight movement, indicating the place where Marie kept her plants, her flowers that were half the joy of her life, and that required so large a quantity of water in the heat of summer.

'Economize! water!' she exclaimed.

'Yes; we can spare no more for luxuries. Without water the animals will die, and worse evils yet may befall. The flowers must suffer first.'

Marie made a little pathetic gesture.

'It will be sad to see them die,' she said. 'Almost like ceasing to feed one's children.'

'Shall I have them taken away?' he said, smiling.

'No. I will have courage. I will keep them while they do not suffer, and when they begin to thirst I will cut them off with my own hand.'

'That is brave.'

She sighed.

'One wants courage in this life, Paolo—

courage, courage! Perhaps that is the quality, of all others, for which we should pray.'

'The smells in the lower part of the town are very bad to-day,' said Don Paolo. 'I have been talking to Menello, our young new doctor. He says it is too late for remedy; it would not be safe in this hot weather.'

'What is he afraid of?' said Marie, in a low tone.

'Oh, cholera, of course. It increases fast on the Mediterranean. At Spezzia it is terrible. One never knows what may happen.'

'And the Bruzzi water has failed!' exclaimed Madame di St. Isidoro. 'And in cholera-times the people must drink the river water! Well, well, God rules all!'

The Priore did not answer for a moment; then he said suddenly:

'By-the-bye, madamina, I have again seen the girl with the face of a Lucca della Robbia angel. It is changed. She has gone through much. It is strangely spiritualized. Who is she? Are you sure that your friends are not here? It must be the fair-haired child who married Eustace Bellingham.'

'I know they are not here. But Paolo, Paolo, it may be his wife. I have never told you, only yesterday I had a long letter from Alice. She told me bad news indeed. That little fair-haired Kitty, whom you admired so much, has left her husband.'

'Left him! Impossible! What misery —and he so fine a fellow!'

'The story is very sad. You know of his old attachment to some one else?'

'Something about it I knew—no names.'

'She, the first love, married, and he was very unhappy. This was when he was here ; and she, your little friend, grew to care for him too much. Some one told him so ; and out of kindness, chivalry, and disappointment, he married her.'

' Yes ; but she was charming. Did they not agree ?'

' Ah ! there is the sad thing. How badly these things are arranged in England ! Judicious parents would have managed all. What have girls to do with love and such follies before they are married ? I have no patience with them ! She was not satisfied ; the first love haunted her, and one fine day she heard it said that he had married her for charity because she cared for him, she could not bear it, and she fled away. They have searched far and wide. At last he discovers what it is to possess a wife, when she is lost. He is in despair, and she will not return. Oh, do you really think that she is here ?'

' After what you say, I am quite sure of it. I have seen her twice.'

' Where? What was she doing?'

' She was in the worst part of the town, nursing a sickly child while the mother took much-needed rest—that was the first time; the second, I saw her kneeling in St. Onofrio.'

' I must find her !'

' Yes. Poor foolish child,' said the Priore thoughtfully, ' she has much to learn.'

' You will teach her ?' said Marie, looking at him lovingly.

' Her own heart will teach her,' he answered. ' Even the path of the sternest self-sacrifice, of the deepest devotion to God's law, must not be wilfully chosen.'

' You would send her back ?'

' Duty before sacrifice.'

Marie recognised the truth of his words, and bowed her head.

'If I can help you, you will let me know?' she said.

'Yes. Find her out, madamina ; win her to come and see you. Poor little soul! And now I must go. I am to meet Menello at the hospital this afternoon. There is much to arrange ; this failure of the Bruzzi water is a very serious calamity.'

When Madame di St. Isidoro was left alone, she began to wonder how she should find Kitty. Santa Chiara was by no means a small place ; she conjectured that Lady Bellingham would not have gone to an hotel. In the great heat of the weather she felt unequal to much search. An inspiration seized her. There was one shop where English Tauchnitz were sold ; there, if anywhere, she might hear news of her. No Englishwoman could remain long in Santa Chiara without Tauchnitz—that was self-evident. Marie dressed, and started at once, even in the blazing heat of the day.

She kept on the shady side of the streets, and was glad when she reached the Strada Reale—a long, principal street of the town, where the houses were all built over stone arcades, in the fashion of Genoa.

Emerging from a shop in this street she met her son, and the new doctor of whom he had already frequently spoken. Marie was curious about him; she had very seldom heard Don Paolo speak so enthusiastically of anyone.

She made a little bow, and the Priore saw her, stopped, and introduced his companion —Ettore Menello.

Marie was pleased with his looks. He was a young, slender man, with square shoulders, and the look of having seen military service; he was very dark, with black hair closely cut, a fiercely waxed moustache, and large brown eyes which were restless and brilliant when excited, but with all the soft glowing fervour of Italian eyes when he chose.

'You are abroad in the fiercest heat of the day, madame,' he began. 'Don Paolo and I have business that cannot be delayed; but who that could help it would face this?'

'My business is not urgent,' said Marie, with her winning smile; 'but I seek a friend, and friendship is impatient.'

'The little white Englishwoman,' said Don Paolo, smiling, in explanation.

'Ah! the little white lady, so the people call her. You seek her? Do you know her?' he said eagerly.

'If she is the same person whom I believe her to be, I should know her well. How long has she been here? How did she obtain that *sobriquet?*'

'She came three weeks ago—about the

10th of August. She lodges in Via San Vitale; she goes about among the poor—they like her much; they think she is come to help them through the bad season.'

'You know her?'

'I have met her twice. She was nursing a sick child. It was the house to which I took you'—and he turned towards the Priore. 'The child died, the little white lady was sorry; she wept, and her tears made the people love her. I can show you where she lives, madame; but it is a quarter in which I am not very popular.' And he smiled broadly, showing all his white teeth.

They walked along the streets together. Marie did not ask what he meant—she was too courteous; but she wondered.

It was actually painful to leave those deep-shadowed arcades and to emerge into the blaze of the sun. Dr. Menello led the way. The streets through which they passed were very dirty—foul with decayed cabbage-stalks and vegetable refuse of all kinds—they had a heavy sickening smell. They came suddenly on the market-place; it was a picturesque scene. The market was roofed and supported by tall slender pillars; two or three steps led up to a raised platform, and on these brown half-clad children played, and a few old women sat. It was an idle time of day.

In a conspicuous place was one stall at which two peasant-women were carrying on an active business. The stall was covered with great water-melons; everyone who passed by stopped and bought one of the sweet dripping slices, and went on his way refreshed.

A low hiss greeted the young doctor. Marie looked astonished—the market-women were hissing him. An old hag crouched up on the steps muttered an '*Accidente.*'

He only smiled a little.

'Unfortunately,' he said, 'it has somehow got abroad that I have been trying to get the sale of water-melons controlled. It will be dangerous soon ; but they don't like it. Come, Fiammetta!' he exclaimed, springing up the steps and approaching the market-women, 'give me a slice. How much ? Fifty *centesimi !* For shame, for shame! Never mind. I will ruin myself for the sake of goodwill.'

'Ah! when the Signor Dottore tastes and sees how delicious it is, he will repent of his little game,' said the woman sullenly.

'Come, come, my friend! we will say no more about it till the time comes, eh ?'

'Times are bad enough without taking such little profit as this from us,' she said, as he turned away. 'So, he has not given

it up—the wretch! the traitor!' and again
the slight hiss followed him.

'The beautiful fresh fruit will soon be
rank poison,' he said, as they walked on
together. 'But I think we have time yet.'

They came into a little piazza, which was
half filled by the marble basin of the
Bruzzi water. The work was an ancient
sculpture of Niccola Pisano, and very
beautiful. Alas! the costly marbles lay
baking and discolouring in the sun ; the
masks and lions' heads, from which clear
streams were wont to fall in delicious
abundance, were dry.

Menello, who seemed to get more absorbed in thought and less inclined to talk
every moment, went up quickly to the
basin and peered down into it long and
anxiously. With an iron pole which lay
against the wall he touched the mud, and
again peered down.

The mud grows hard and baked,' he said. 'Not one drop is rising from the spring. Well, well—patience!'

Presently they came to Via San Vitale. The houses were large, tall, and fine, though in the midst of a bad and low neighbourhood.

'Here lives the little white lady,' said Menello, smiling; 'and here I must, I fear, leave you, madame.'

'You will come and see me,' said Marie rather eagerly; 'you will always find me in the evening.'

'If I may do myself so much honour.'

He raised his hat with a flourishing sweep, and went away at a brisk pace.

CHAPTER IX.

THE Priore came home late. Madame di St. Isidoro was standing by her flowers—the poor flowers that were doomed. She had opened the windows wide and the doors, in hopes of introducing a little cool air; but the white curtains of the room never stirred, not a leaf moved—the air that did come in was heat rather than air. The flowers hung their heads, their leaves drooped; the dry earth was cracked and crumbling. At this hour Marie was wont to deluge them with water—to watch them drinking it in with greedy rapture, their leaves freshening, the sweet life reviving in every drooping blossom.

As she watched, large tears she could not suppress gathered in her eyes; it was terrible to her to let them die like this. Don Paolo laid his hand on her shoulder and made her start, and then laugh, while she surreptitiously brushed away the tears.

'You have surprised a poor Hagar mourning over her Ishmael,' she said.

'Come, come—your resolution! They are not suffering yet, they are only thirsty, as many other forms of life are thirsty just now. The people who have lived on the Bruzzi water for so long are almost in a state of rebellion because they have to go to the river for water; and what is to become of the last remnant of cleanliness! Who can tell? Well, mother, was it Lady Bellingham, or not?'

Marie moved away from her flowers.

' Come and sit down, Paolo,' she said. 'I have coffee for you; and while you drink it I will tell you. Yes, it is a most extraordinary fact that it is Lady Bellingham—the same little Kitty Brown-Clifford whom you admired for the sweetness of her face.'

' Where did you find her?'

' In that old house they call the Casa Rossa ; it is very large and very bare—the rooms so large and high that they are cool. Little Kitty glides about them all dressed in white, looking so childish and so lonely. When she first saw me she gave a little scream of recognition, and ran forward eagerly and kissed me ; then she became very pale, and stood quite silently before me with her head hanging down.

' " Perhaps you would not let me kiss you," she said, " if you knew what I have done."

' "I know you have left your husband," I said, as severely as I could; and then, for it was like speaking to a child, I said: "What does your mamma say to that?" '

' And did she tell you her reasons?'

' Oh yes; she had her reasons all ready. From her point of view her conduct is sublime; from his, naturally, it is madness. How shall we reconcile the two?   Shall we write and tell them she is here?'

'Not yet.   Let us try and win from her the atonement she ought to make.   If we fail——'

' But you never fail, Paolo mine,' said his mother lovingly.   'With you it is only a matter of time.   By-the-bye, do you know that Ursel has come back?'

'No.   Have you seen him?'

' I saw him in the street to-day, and spoke to him.   I do not think you would know him, he is so changed.   He looks radiant—

so prosperous, so brilliant. I never saw a human face with such a glow of happy life shining over it.'

'Good Ursel! I shall be glad to see him again.'

'I asked him whether he had come to stay here, and he answered for a short time only. He is going to America in the beginning of November. Meanwhile, he has gone to his old home on the Roman road.'

'You heard that he was free from his *impresario?*'

'Yes, but not how it came to pass.'

'By the same hand that gave him Melu-sina—English, of course.'

'Sir Eustace?'

'No; for lack of means, not will. I fancy it was his brother-in-law.'

'The little man who married Georgina, whom I never liked? But surely he did not care for Ursel?'

'I cannot say. I only think,' answered Don Paolo. 'And much as you may look down on that unattractive little Englishman, madamina, let me tell you that I never saw anything like his devotion to his brother-in-law. There is nothing more beautiful in life than a man's love for his faithful friend.'

'You are always right,' she said affectionately. 'What, going already? No peace, no rest?'

'Have I not had at least half an hour's rest? And to be with you is always peace.'

It was very rarely he used words like that. They brought the warm, tender glow to her heart that few had power to bring there now.

'I shall try and see Ursel as soon as I can,' he said, as he was leaving the room. 'I am anxious to see my old friend, and to judge for myself how triumphs agree with him.'

' Surely you saw that here ?'

' Ah, this little place is not the great world. Applause from lesser men is success; applause from the master-minds is triumph. Ursel bore success very philosophically; he had not tasted the more intoxicating draught.'

' *Au revoir!*' she answered, waving her fingers, and going back in her solitude to wistful watching of her poor drooping flowers.

Kitty Bellingham could not have told the reason why she had come to Santa Chiara, if she had been asked to do so. She was drifting about as the waves of destiny chose to drift her, giving little thought as to her destination. Some fancy, some hope that it would soften the never-ceasing aching of her heart to be once more in scenes hallowed by association may have guided her, but she came very listlessly.

Again, it was almost without volition of her own that she went to the Casa Rossa. She found herself travelling with the owner and his wife. They were courteous to her. Her forbore to smoke when he saw that it disturbed her. The good wife gave her a band-box on which to rest her weary feet, and offered her chocolate and unsavoury slabs of Bologna sausage; and by-and-by, when she spoke of a lodging, offered to take her in, and give her the large empty rooms in which she had established herself.

There she stayed, sometimes for hours together pacing up and down the waxed floors, sometimes leaning out of the windows with wistful blue eyes always straining upwards—not into the busy, picturesque life of the narrow street below, but upwards, from whence alone the help would come—

the help that must come to teach her how to face the life that lay before her.

The help came thus at last. A little crying child hurt in the street. Kitty carried it home, and found herself in the midst of work to do—poor people content with very little, but needing that little just to live; bad times, sickness, improvidence; little laughing black-eyed children rolling in the dust one day, the next hungry, fever-stricken.

Kitty began to work daily amongst the poor; doing more and more till her life was much like that of a Sister. The help had come; the hard misery began to melt round her heart; the passionate love she felt for the husband she had left, seemed no longer the torture but the strength of her life.

The heat grew greater day by day, and the sufferings of the people increased. The river was far off, and they were lazy, ease-loving creatures; it was cruel when the day's work was done to have the long extra tramp to fetch water—it was a bitter grievance to them.

When Kitty went next time to see Madame di St. Isidoro, she found her sitting crying so bitterly that she had to turn consoler.

'What is it? What is it?' she cried in her gentle, pathetic voice. 'How can I comfort you?'

Then Marie smiled, and even laughed like a true Frenchwoman through her tears, and put back the pretty gray hair from her brow.

'It is most childish to cry,' she said. 'You, with great living sorrows, may laugh at me. It is only that with my own hand I have cut my flowers to save them from dying of thirst. Ah, dear little friend, I also have had my great sorrows in my day, and I have lived through them. And now, perhaps, you can hardly understand; but the little sorrows are reflections of the great ones—stones thrown into still depths which rouse up and stir the pain which only sleeps and never dies.'

'Does it never die—never?' said Kitty wistfully—she was not thinking of herself, but of Eustace—and Madame di St. Isidoro shook her head.

'Ursel spoke the truth,' she said. 'The grass grows over our graves, but the graves are there.'

Kitty did not answer. The words brought back to her the whole bright scene. She glanced round the room. Once more she could see it peopled with those dear faces that were all the world to her. She could hear Ursel's quiet voice. It was so vivid that she started when Marie spoke again.

'You think me very foolish to cry for flowers? Do you not?'

'It is the little things, not the great ones, that make one cry,' answered Kitty simply. 'But why have you cut them all? They must have been so beautiful.'

'They drank so much.'

'Ah, I understand. Well, let us make the best of them;' and with dexterous fingers she began to arrange the poor cut flowers in a vase. Before the task was over, Marie was laughing over it in her own bright way.

When Kitty left the Palazzo St. Isidoro to go home, the feeling of desolation was upon her very strongly. The dread of going back to those great empty rooms, to sit through the evening with no one to whom to speak, nothing to do but to read the books which brought her no forgetfulness, for the concentration of her thoughts was such that

she could understand nothing that she read.
A despairing feeling came over her.   Could
she carry out the task she had set herself?
Had she overrated her own strength?

She turned her restless steps out of the
town.   She thought she would go a little
way along the Roman road.

It was not deserted; all the weary toilers,
men and women, from the town would be on
their way to or from the river.   It was
growing late; the fierce sun was going down
in a sky which blazed like molten brass.
The heat was intense, and heavy, unwhole-
some smells rose up from the burning
streets.   Over the distant country hovered
a kind of mist, which spoke of heat, not of
fresh, damp dew.

Kitty did not walk far; she sat down on a
stone bench by the wayside, listlessly watching the passers-by — pitying the brown
mules as they strained with their heavily-

laden carts up the steep ascent; pitying the children and very old men and women as they staggered homewards with the jar or pitcher of water; then idly admiring the handsome girls who came swinging down the hill, each with her big earthen water-jar poised on her head. Some of them burst into song as they passed. A baker's boy, scantily clothed, but beautiful as Apollo, sang in a lovely tenor voice, swinging his long, shiny, brown loaves in time as he poured a passionate love-song into the air.

Kitty listened till the last sweet notes died away; then slowly, wearily, she rose and began to turn homewards, when a sudden familiar voice broke upon her ear.

'Is it possible? Do I not dream? Is it you, Lady Bellingham?'

Mechanically she held out her hand.

'It is, Monsieur Ursel,' she said, 'I myself.'

' Ah.'

The long-drawn syllable, the look of astonishment—half-pain, half-joy — on his face, made her start.

' I am here only for a short time. I—I— am travelling,' she faltered.

' I see. I know. Ah, thank God I have found you !' he exclaimed with intense earnestness. ' It will save his life from wreck.'

' What do you mean?' she cried, the words terrifying her. ' Of whom do you speak ?'

' Of your husband, Lady Bellingham ; of the man whom in all the world I love the best. You would hardly know him if you saw him now, he is so changed. He has grown so thin, so wan.'

' Has he been ill ?'

' Ill ? Yes. And I think his heart is broken !'

Kitty struggled hard to master the sob

that would rise in her throat. She knew that he was heart-broken, but, alas! she did not believe that it was for lack of her. She sat down again on the bench from which she had risen—she could not stand.

About three or four paces away from them was a little café ; it had been so quiet that she had not noticed its existence, but now a sound of loud voices and uproar and crash began to be heard from within. Kitty was too much absorbed to hear it.

'Monsieur Ursel,' she said, 'tell me what you can, what you will, about them all. I have heard no news for so long,' she said feverishly.

He leant against the wall beside her ; he took off his hat and passed his long fingers through his hair.

'I saw him last in Eaton Square,' he said. 'I went to bid them farewell ; they had been so good to me—how good I cannot

tell you—words fail me. I saw Miss Bellingham; she told me that at last he consented to leave home. The suspense was
killing him, she said ; but at last——’

‘ Where was he going ?’

‘ I will tell you. He had just returned
from Dover.’

‘ From Dover, ah ?’

‘ Yes ; he had traced you there. He
went full of hope ; he came back half dead
with despair—— Ah! what can be the
matter ?’

He broke off so suddenly that Kitty,
much startled, sprang to her feet.

Two men, evidently in the most un-
governable rage, had burst out of the little
café, followed by a crowd of eager men,
uttering quick, frightened remonstrances.
Just outside the porch the two antagonists
turned upon each other ; the foremost, a
big heavy man of fifty, rushed upon the

younger—unfortunately his own son—and struck him savagely in the face.

Kitty could not control a sharp cry, for she saw the younger man suddenly draw backwards, as if for a spring, and the sharp glittering flash of a long knife cut the air.

A dozen hands stretched out were withdrawn; the remonstrances increased in vehemence as the spectators shrank back from the vicinity of the dangerous weapon. The lad was beside himself; having missed his first stroke, he was gathering himself together for another and more fatal one, when Ursel, with one bound, reached the spot. He seized his arm, he fought wildly for the knife; the young man turned all his fury upon him, hitting him frantically before he could be overpowered.

The father, subdued by what had taken place, stood shaking from head to foot;

while the spectators half forced, half carried the still raving son back into the café.

Ursel was standing quite still in the middle of the street. With his left hand he had wound his handkerchief rapidly round the right hand, the blood was pouring through it, pouring in red streams on the dusty road.

'Are you much hurt?' asked Kitty, trembling from head to foot as she came up to him. 'Only tell me what I can do.'

'It is nothing—a trifle,' he answered. 'If only, perhaps, Menello——'

'Yes, yes; he will come at once,' said Kitty.

She held out her hand, and made him sit on the bench, then glanced at him again. He was not looking at her—he was looking away into space, and there was something strange in the look of his eyes that terrified her. What did it mean?

She turned, and ran for Dr. Menello—ran with the wonderful swift running that made her old companions say in the old days that little Kitty ran like the wind.

CHAPTER X.

LADY BELLINGHAM found Ettore Menello much sooner than she could have dared to hope. He was just leaving the hospital, and Don Paolo was with him; they were talking earnestly together.

Kitty told her story breathlessly. Menello waited for no details, but dashed into his surgery, re-issued with needful articles, and ran up the road looking right and left for a carriage.

Don Paolo followed him. Lady Bellingham would fain have done so also, but her knees were failing her ; the objects on which her eyes looked were dancing round her. She was afraid of fainting, so she went slowly to Palazzo St. Isidoro, which was nearer than her own home, and begged leave to wait there, her account of the accident making Marie as anxious as she was herself.

Don Paolo and Menello were fortunate enough to find a carriage, and in an incredibly short time they had arrived on the spot.

Ursel had not moved ; he was leaning back on the stone bench, with his head against the wall. A little crowd was standing round him chattering about the doctor's coming, and discussing whether it would be better to get him home or to leave him where he was.

A glance at Ursel's face made the young doctor start ; there was a kind of smile on it—a strange, drowsy look—the eyes half-closed. He glanced downwards hastily. The blood was flowing in a slow, steady stream.

Don Paolo saw his glance, and understood. He obeyed every minutest direction, the first being brandy—brandy, as much as they could get down his throat.

Menello bound up the wound there on the spot, speaking in a whisper to his friend: 'All right, we are in time.'

Then between them they carried Ursel, who became gradually unconscious, into the carriage, home, and so to his bed.

'Just in time, only just in time! the man was bleeding to death!' said Menello, with a sigh of relief. 'Who is he? I did not catch the name.'

'Who? Do you not know him? Michel Ursel.'

'Ursel? Santi Apostoli! you do not say so! But this is terrible!'

' Surely you said we were in time !'

' Yes, yes; he will not die. But poor fellow, poor fellow! perhaps he will think it a cruel kindness that we did not let him bleed to death; it is a gentle end.'

' I do not understand.'

Menello gave a quick sigh.

' Patience,' he said. ' Life is hard. Death is more merciful. See, he moves! I shall soon have to resign him into your hands. I can cure wounded bodies; but broken hearts I leave to you.'

' You mean——?'

' Hush ! Speak low. The tendons of the wrist are severed. He will never play again.'

' Ah !'

Don Paolo hid his face in his hands. It seemed too terrible to be true. It is not death that is sad; it is life.

Menello was bending over his patient.

When he looked up again the room was growing dark. The short Southern twilight was at an end.

Menello, whose movements were sharp and alert, came back to his side and spoke low.

'I think he will sleep now,' he said. 'He has lost a great deal of blood. It is only exhaustion at present. If we can keep off worse consequences he will be all right soon. Would you not wish to go? You can do no good. He must be kept quite quiet: and you have so much to do.'

'And you?'

Menello glanced anxiously at the bed.

'I have a thousand engagements,' he said: but I will keep none of them. I shall not leave him to-night.'

'You think there is still danger?'

'I do not like his looks. I am not sure that he is as insensible as he seems; and—

the man has seen his ship go down before his very eyes.'

' You think he knows?'

Menello nodded.

'Pah! how hot it is !' he exclaimed. ' And how the bad smells of the town reach us even here !'

' You will not sit up all night ?'

'Am I a soldier for nothing? Have I been through two campaigns without learning to sleep soundly sitting, standing, or kneeling if necessary? And here is the luxury of a sofa.'

' To-morrow ?'

'Come early ; I shall want you. I must be off by seven o'clock.'

Don Paolo still lingered.

'Do you want anything? You will let me know?'

' Certainly. Stay ! Send me up the papers and any books you can find downstairs ; and tell the landlady to send up lights. That is all. Good-night.'

The Priore went away, unwilling enough to go, but aware that he could do no good by staying. He went homewards, a weight on his heart such as he had hardly ever felt before. What was to become of Ursel ? How could he bear life bereft of everything that made it joy to live ?

The great door of St. Onofrio stood wide open. He looked in. The broad nave was in deep shadow. Far away the glimmering lamps which hung before the High Altar made the dim arches and pillars into a far perspective doubly long.

He went in. It was cold, with a chill marble freshness. The faint odour of incense lingered on the air. He knelt down and prayed for Ursel — prayed till the perspiration stood on his brow, wrestling for a soul in deadly peril at that hour.

The night drew on. All [the inhabitants of Santa Chiara had gone to rest. It was a breathless night, hot and airless. The moon sailed calmly through a cloudless sky.

Menello had taken off his coat, had thrown himself back on the little hard-backed sofa, and had fallen asleep.

Far away the great deep-toned bell of St. Onofrio clanged out two o'clock; nearer at hand jangled a shrill convent bell.

The moon came in, and her light lay square like a white sheet on the floor, making all shadows black and distinct.

Menello slept; but he slept the light slumber of an accustomed nurse. There was a little sound scarcely audible from Ursel's bed—a sigh, a very faint sigh—but it was enough; he was on his feet at once, and bending over his patient.

'Ah!' he exclaimed; 'I was right then, after all!'

He spoke almost vehemently, and with rapid fingers struck a match and lit candles in the room; as he did so, the blood was dripping from his hand.

The light revealed to him Ursel's face, his eyes fixed upon him with a glare so terrible that he saw there was no time to lose. He rang the bell fiercely, violently. He threw himself upon his patient—the unhappy Ursel had torn off his bandages; the wound was open again; another few minutes and nothing could have saved him.

The landlord of the house and his son answered the summons. Obeying Menello, they secured Ursel while he again bound up the wound. It was a fearful moment. Ursel fought hard, his face was distorted with despair; he even attempted to tear at the bandages with his teeth; and when the work was done and he was safely bound down, the sobbing, panting breathing almost convulsed him.

Menello made the men leave the room, and he sat down by Ursel and took his left hand; the fingers closed on it as in a vice, the nails entering his flesh.

' Ursel,' he said, ' my poor friend !'

He was breathing hard himself — the exertion had been great—the fear of failure worse still.

The wounded man groaned deeply, and muttered words between his teeth.

' Monsieur Ursel,' said Menello, ' it grieves me deeply to treat you like this. Come, be a man !'

' Five minutes! only five minutes longer! Why did you stop me? What right had you to interfere ?' and with wild words he cursed him.

'Five minutes between you and hell!' said Menello quietly.

He did not look at Ursel, he was busy washing the blood-stains from his hands; he could hear the quivering start.

'And what if I think any alternative better than life?'

'Must I not think also of myself and my own responsibility in the matter?'

Again the deep terrible curses.

Menello turned round suddenly.

'Are you the only man in the world,' he exclaimed, 'who has lost his all?'

'My loss is a world's loss!' cried Ursel, his voice sounding like a cry.

'True; but have you never heard of great men being cut off when their services were most required? How did Beethoven bear his deafness? Huber his loss of sight? I cannot preach, my friend—I leave that to my betters; but I have seen a man carried off the battle-field with both legs cut off, with a smile on his face! I have seen a widow close the eyes of her last living child! Are you the only man on earth who has been called out to suffer? Tell me,' he exclaimed, suddenly changing his tone, ' does your arm give you much pain?'

' It aches—it aches!'

' You are worn out; you want rest. Can you not summon up courage?'

' I have courage to die.'

' Courage to live is what I want to see. Some philosophy. Come, my friend.'

Still the agonized look remained, the drooping head, the eyes turning from side to side, the wild muttered words.

Later, Menello gave him an opiate; it required force to make him take it, but it was done; and when the gray light of early morning began to dawn, the unhappy Ursel slept at last.

About five o'clock Don Paolo came in. Menello met him in the anteroom, and in a few words told him what had passed.

'See, Priore,' he said, 'I will now take some rest; but you must watch—not for one moment must we relax our vigilance.'

Menello threw himself on the sofa, and at once fell asleep.

The Priore sat by Ursel, watching him with sad eyes. He presented a terrible spectacle—the bed-clothes drenched with blood, the hair clotted and tangled, his face drawn and haggard, as if with the sickness of long months.

As the clock struck seven, Menello rose from his sleep, refreshed, bright, and alert. He came up to the sleeping man, looked at him earnestly, and felt his pulse.

'He will sleep another two or three hours,' he whispered to the Priore; 'can you stay?'

'Yes; I shall be here when he wakes.'

'No—not that. I will send in a Sister; when he first wakes, he will want food and water and all comforts; afterwards go to him. I shall soon be back.'

'And then?' said Don Paolo, touching the long strips of linen which bound poor Ursel so effectively.

'We will see when he wakes. Adieu! I will be back as soon as I can.'

By-and-by a quiet Sister came in, with a gentle motherly face. Don Paolo knew her well.

'I am glad it is you, Suora Agnese,' he said.

She nodded, and sat down, folding her hands in the long sleeves of her habit. Long hours passed; then, presently, with a deep, slow sigh, Ursel awoke.

Suora Agnese made a quick sign to Don Paolo, who placed himself out of sight.

'Ah! awake at last,' she said cheerily; and she went on talking quietly and gently to him, sponging with warm water, softly brushing out his wild hair.

Ursel lay all the while speechless, as if in a strange, misty dream. Once or twice he tried to move his hands, but not being able to do so did not seem to disturb him.

When Suora Agnese had done her work she beckoned to Don Paolo.

'Come and sit here, Signor Priore,' she said, 'while I go and bring something to eat.'

She went away downstairs, and Don Paolo came and sat down by the bed. Ursel looked at him with strange eyes; then he said, very slowly:

' " The tendons of the wrist are severed; he will never play again." '

The Priore started. He had, then, heard Menello's words, low as they had been spoken. He had heard them, but they had been no news to him; they had only con- firmed what he already knew.

'God has withdrawn the gift he gave,' said Don Paolo softly.

A fierce flash came over Ursel's face, then died away ; the effect of the opiate was not yet exhausted. He spoke again—so low that the Priore was forced to bend down to hear :

' " The tendons of the wrist are severed; he will never play again." '

The Sister brought soup, and Ursel drank it, and by-and-by he slept again. When Menello came in in the blazing heat of the afternoon, he was satisfied with the con- dition of his patient. The dressing of the wound brought ease and comfort.

Don Paolo gave a long sigh of relief.

' The worst is over,' he said. ' Will you not unbind him now ?'

' A little patience,' said Menello ; ' I dare not yet.'

And he was right, for the night which followed was far worse than the first ; and when Don Paolo and the doctor looked each other in the face in the blue light of the early morning, it was to thank God that it was over, and that exhaustion had followed upon those fearful paroxysms of despair.

Some days passed, and by slow degrees Ursel began to grow better—to grow better in spite of the agony which threatened his reason. His hand was healing, health was returning ; and now Don Paolo began his work. He pleaded with him as a father pleading with a beloved son. He spoke of Love, and Mercy, and Hope. He told of sufferings far greater than human imagination can reach, till the hard strain seemed to melt, and some kind of softening light to steal over the sick man's eyes.

'Now you will unloose those terrible bonds?' said the Priore entreatingly to Menello.

'Does Ursel wish it?'

'I cannot tell—he never rebels against them now ; but it is piteous, it is horrible to see him bound.'

'If he rebelled against it, it would be a better sign,' said Menello thoughtfully. 'Then I might not hesitate.'

'But as it is?'

'I think he may feel them a protection against himself.'

'But you say he could walk now if he tried?'

'Yes ; he is strong enough.'

'Ettore, trust to me in this. Loose him ; let him be free. He cannot harm himself with so many near. We will redouble our precautions.'

Menello yielded. He loosed all the bandages. Ursel was free again.

The wounded man was still strangely silent. He would listen earnestly to all Don Paolo said, but he answered nothing—not even the acquiescence to the words of resignation his friend yearned so to hear. While he listened, his eyes were always restlessly wandering round the room, as though seeking something that he should never find again.

'It is all right—he is perfectly calm and still,' said Don Paolo.

As the days went by, he was forced away by his various duties; and one day it chanced that neither of the friends was able to be there. That hour's interval was enough. When they met again it was with white faces, and hearts full of poignant anxiety. Ursel was gone; and nowhere, far or near, could they find a trace of him.

CHAPTER XI.

THE Priore returned home to Palazzo St. Isidoro one night, with a look of care and depression on his face that his mother had never seen equalled before.

'No news ?' she said sorrowfully.

'Nothing—nothing ;' and, to her consternation, she saw that his hands were shaking almost as if with ague.

'You will never be able to preach to-night,' she said anxiously. 'You must rest, Paolo.'

'It will do me good,' he answered, with a

forced smile. ' I am altogether unhinged. The concentration of thought will brace me again. What o'clock is it, madamina?'

' It is seven. You have an hour yet.'

' Ah! then get me coffee or a *bouillon*—I care not which — and send it to my room.'

' Your sermon is not then prepared?'

' Not a word of it.'

Marie made no remark. She followed her son into his room, and saw him sit down on one of the hard wooden chairs. The room was utterly devoid of comfort. A deal table, bare floor, no stove or means of warming it; on one wall a tall, beautifully-carved crucifix, on the other deal shelves full of books.

Marie went away to fetch the soup. She carried it up to him with her own hands. She found the Priore seated exactly as she had left him, one hand supporting his forehead, the other hanging by his side—an attitude almost of despondency.

'You do not get on,' she said, timidly laying one gentle hand on his shoulder.

'I cannot,' he answered. 'I am over-whelmed with remorse, with self-reproach. How can I preach to others? I who have failed so terribly!'

Marie came and gently put the food before him.

'Courage!' she said. 'You have been too incessantly successful, *mon ami*, so that you have forgotten how to bear failure.'

She spoke in a light, caressing tone.

He looked up at her sorrowfully.

'Perhaps you are right, mother,' he said. 'It is all my fault, my want of humility.'

'Come and eat now,' said Madame di St. Isidoro, with her French quickness of speech. 'The principal thing is to be ready to go up into the pulpit when the time comes.   As for what you have to say, the words will come with the occasion.'

Don Paolo raised the soup to his lips, then put it down untasted.   He felt as if he could not swallow it.   Suddenly he took it up again, saying, with a smile, 'Come, come! this also is a form of self-indulgence,' and drank it down.

Marie said no more.   She went downstairs, put on her bonnet, and started by herself for church.

The heat was intense; the pavement seemed to blister her feet.   She glanced up at the sky with a great longing.   Would the sweet, wholesome rain never come again?

A flight of broad, shallow steps led up to the façade of St. Onofrio.   The great west doors were set wide open to allow the hot outside air to come in and break the vault-like cold of this great solemn Lombard church.

It was still early, but people were coming in, anxious to secure seats in the nave. Marie suddenly perceived among them the little slender figure of Lady Bellingham, and she hastened to join her. Kitty went half-way up the nave, pausing almost under the twisted columns that supported the great square pulpit. She had come for counsel and help; she wanted to hear every word.

They sat and knelt long waiting, while the shadows grew dimmer and the yellow Altar lights glimmered more brightly. Slowly the great church filled.

There was a heavy weight hanging over the town—a dulness, a depression that could hardly be accounted for. It seemed as if the lamp of life burnt at a low ebb, there was so much inertia and exhaustion everywhere.

A great sea of faces turned upwards as Don Paolo appeared in the pulpit, turned with one accord towards him. Looking down on them, he knew that the words would be sent to him, that to-night he would be a messenger from heaven. Some souls in need might be strengthened on their weary way.

The Priore was suffering keenly; he reproached himself, believing that he had been altogether mistaken in his treatment of Ursel. He had spoken to him of patience, of love, of comfort; but was his soul ripe for it? Should he not have appealed, not to the man's weakness, but his strength, demanding of him acceptance of his doom? In his vast experience of great sorrows, he had known the great truth that submission must come first, the bowing down, the cry of 'Fiat voluntas Tua!' and after that came the time to speak of comfort and of patience. But that breaking down of will, that lying prostrate at the foot of the Cross—that had never come to Ursel. He had spoken of comfort where there could be no comfort; he had spoken softly when his words should have been relentless, implacable. Learn first that this is the will of God. There is no escape—none. This that has come upon you is the unchangeable fiat of your Maker.

It was not the first time that he had failed thus. His heart was overcharged with sympathy ; it ached so painfully for the wounds he saw. He lived in them, suffered in them ; and in bitter remorse now he saw that he himself had sympathized with that rebellion—had felt it was hard, too hard to bear—and he had lost Ursel.

He read out in his deep musical voice, every word of which rang through the church, 'Woe unto him that striveth with his Maker. Let the potsherd strive with the potsherds of the earth. Shall the clay say to Him that fashioned it, What makest Thou?'

Then he began to speak, and the listening people hung on his words. They were different from what they were accustomed to hear from him ; this was no sermon against sin and evil, such as had often stirred their consciences and influenced their lives ; no message of consolation, no exhortation to prayer, penitence, or hope. He put before them in great soul-stirring words the mightiness of God, the omnipotence of the Creator of heaven, and earth, and sea, and he called upon the creatures to bow down to their Creator, and to accept of His hand the light and the darkness, the good and the evil of the life that was not theirs but His.

As he spoke, there came over all those

soft pleasure-loving Italians a dim sense of the littleness of man, a momentary glance at a vast magnificence which had not come home to them. As he went on, some of the simpler ones among his hearers shuddered as if they could not understand. What was this self-abnegation of which he spoke? this absolute surrender of will to God? The age was soft, he said; it could not cope with this idea of unhesitating, unqualified obedience. Duty was wrapped up in sentiment. Men talked of love and comfort, men asked for help and implored in broken words for happiness, when duty was enough for all, and the first law of life obedience. Don Paolo knew his people well; he knew the strange national character, so full of complications, both from habit and temperament, fatalist and absolutely self-indulgent, and yet having within it a capability of reaching a height of self-abnegation and asceticism no other has surpassed.

As he poured out his words, suddenly his eyes fell on one anxious pleading face gazing up at him—it was that of Kitty Bellingham. An agonized thought came over him. Here also was one straying out of the path of duty. Should he lose this soul also, as perhaps he had lost that other despairing soul of whom he hardly dared to think ?

The thought quickened his words. The people shrank; it was as if a great map of life were laid before them, and the things they loved so well and looked upon as the main good of the world, were shown them in the proportion they would assume when looked down upon from heaven.

The burning words sank into their hearts. Kitty bowed her head between her hands, and trembled from head to foot—a new and searching light had burst in upon her.

The sermon was over, the congregation all dispersed, and still she knelt on, trembling.

At last Marie touched her gently.

'Come home with me,' she said; 'come home, and rest!'

Kitty raised herself; she could hardly have walked without the help of her friend. Marie understood little of the feelings which were thus overpowering her; she was puzzled by the intense agitation. She led her indoors, and placed her by the open window, and gently fanned her.

'Poor child — poor little thing!' she said.

Presently the door opened, and Don Paolo came in. The light shone on his grave and exhausted face; he did not know that Kitty was there.

She rose to her feet with a little cry, stretching out her hands with the action of a child groping in the dark.

'Tell me what to do!' she cried. 'I thought I was right! Has it been all wrong? all wilful self-seeking? I am in the dark—I cannot see which way to turn! Show me the path of duty!'

Don Paolo answered solemnly:

'Those whom God hath joined together, let not man put asunder.'

'But he did not love me!' her voice rose up in a cry. 'I thought of him—of his happiness—before all!'

'You sacrificed your duty to your God to that false idol men call happiness.'

'Speak gently to her, Paolo,' said Marie imploringly. 'You will break her heart.'

But Kitty turned from her tender hands.

'No, no!' she cried; 'do not spare me!

I hunger—I pant for truth! Have I sinned in doing this thing?'

' You have sinned ; and this sin of yours may be laid to his charge.'

' No, no!'

' Gently, Paolo, gently!' whispered his mother.

He bowed his head. He gave one glance of pity at the prostrate head hidden on Marie's breast, then went away, and left them together.

CHAPTER XII.

KITTY lay awake all that night, tossing painfully from side to side. The knowledge that the course she had taken had been, not the generous self-sacrifice she had deemed it. but a wilful and wrong exercise of free-will, had come upon her with all the shock of a revelation; and the longer she thought of it, the more was the bitter truth burnt into her brain.

She left her bed, she paced up and down her rooms in her restless misery. How true the uncompromising words of the

Priore were, came more and more home to her as she realized the agony it would be to her to return, to humiliate herself—she, the unloved wife, to confess herself in the wrong, and sue to be taken home again and forgiven !

All her life passed before her; all that she had gone through in that home which had been happiness and misery combined. Her morbid nature exaggerated her own faults and defects till she grew into the belief that it was her own want of attraction that had alienated her husband, and that the self-consciousness from which she had suffered so keenly had been nothing but vanity.

The next morning she telegraphed to Castleford, asking whether Sir Eustace were there.

The day during which Kitty waited for an answer seemed endless; yet when it came at last, she could hardly summon up courage enough to tear open the envelope.

The answer was, that Sir Eustace was yachting—his present address uncertain ; all letters were to be forwarded to Lady Bellingham, at the Hotel dell' Arno, Florence.

Her mother-in-law was then in Italy—within one day's journey from her. Kitty almost shrank from showing the telegram to her friend, afraid of the advice that was sure to follow ; but though she might shrink and procrastinate, she was determined in character, and what she considered right she would do, let it cost her what it might.

She knew what the counsel would be before the words were spoken. She must go to her husband's mother ; she must not delay the reconciliation a day longer than was necessary.

Lady Bellingham had established herself in Florence alone. At the last moment Alice had accompanied her brother. He seemed to cling to her companionship, and her mother did not want her. She was tired of her unequal spirits and somewhat broken health. She fancied that when her son and daughter would both rejoin her at Florence, late in the autumn, they would have regained peace, and resigned themselves to the inevitable. And, meanwhile, she made herself very comfortable—made friends with several of the English residents at Florence, with whom she took long drives into the country after the heat of the day; and she was inclined to think that all was for the best, and that with Kitty all the discordant elements of the family circle would by degrees disperse and vanish.

She was so thoroughly selfish a woman,

that when all about her were outwardly calm and at peace, she was perfectly content, neither seeing nor caring for the pain and suffering that were not actually apparent.

Lord and Lady Austen arrived in Florence about the middle of September. The heat was so great that they determined to stay there, and to give up all further travelling until it should be cooler.

It was a great pleasure to Lady Bellingham to meet Marion again; she had always felt for her an affection and admiration she had never felt for anyone else. It was true that she had ruthlessly changed all the tenor of her life, but that was in her nature; apart from that, and now that it had all receded into the past, the old affection came back stronger than ever.

Marion's sweet face was still worn and tired; but there was a look upon it that no one had ever seen before — a look of rest and peace, of a great content—and she was more beautiful than ever.

Lady Bellingham had not seen her more than three times before she knew better than if she had been told that May's weary hunted life had found its anchor at last, and that the great, unselfish, self-sacrificing love which had waited for her so long had found its full reward. To Austen the highest, most perfect reward of all was to see that he made his wife perfectly happy.

So it was; and now and then a selfish pang of envy for her son would flit across Lady Bellingham's mind. But it did not dwell there; there was too much self-reproach in the thought, and self-reproach was a sentiment that she would by no means admit.

One afternoon she came back late from

one of the country drives that were her great pleasure and refreshment. It had been so hot all day that she felt fatigued and languid.

Lady Bellingham was going slowly up-stairs, the active waiters following her with parasol and dust-cloak, when, to her astonishment, her maid met her, running to meet her with an excitement in her manner that altogether metamorphosed that dignified in-dividual. She had been long enough in the family to enter fully into its troubles.

'My lady, my lady!' she cried; 'her ladyship has returned at last. She is in the salon.'

'What do you mean?' exclaimed Lady Bellingham, turning very pale. 'Who do you say is in the salon?'

'Her ladyship is there. Lady Bellingham has come!'

'Impossible!'

In her agitation, Lady Bellingham went eagerly forward ; then stopped, with her hand on the handle of the door, trying to compose her face and determine what she should say first.

When she went in, she saw the slight figure of her daughter-in-law leaning back in a large armchair, in an attitude of extreme lassitude ; but at the sound of her entrance Kitty sprang to her feet, and advanced to meet her with both hands outstretched. Agitation actually deprived her of the power of speaking, and she could only look up in the face of her husband's mother with large eyes and quivering lips.

There was no encouragement to be read in that handsome, implacable face. Lady Bellingham would not see the hands. She swept past her to a chair by the table and sat down.

' This meeting has taken me altogether

by surprise,' she said; and her words sank like lead upon the heart of her hearer. ' In what character have you returned?—as penitent? as suppliant? or simply to arrange business matters?'

Kitty clasped her hands together.

'I have come to ask Eustace to forgive me,' she faltered.

'To forgive you? You speak of it very lightly. He must know first what he has to forgive.'

Kitty was trembling from head to foot.

'I will ask him!' she cried passionately. 'I will appeal to my husband!'

'I beg your pardon,' said Lady Bellingham; 'but that is impossible. My son is not here—he is travelling. I do not even know his address; and,' she added slowly, 'if I did, I would not give it to you.'

'Have you no mercy? You who, of all people, should know best why I left him.'

'I understood that the motive which actuated your most unusual conduct was jealousy. This does not, and cannot, diminish the disgrace that your flight has brought on my son.'

'Disgrace!'

'Perhaps you do not know the meaning of the word?'

Kitty uttered a faint cry.

'Why are you so cruel to me?' she exclaimed. 'I left him because I believed it was for his happiness, and——'

'What has altered your belief?'

Kitty staggered back; she caught hold of a chair to support herself. Lady Bellingham went on:

'You disgraced my son before the world by leaving him as you did. I cannot recommend him to do such an act of weakness as to allow you to return. He would be the laughing-stock of his friends. What have you been doing?   Where have you been?'

'I have been at Santa Chiara.   It was Don Paolo who bade me come back to my husband.'

'He did not know what he was advising,' said Lady Bellingham.   'You must accept the position you made for yourself.'

'Not from you,' said Kitty, her spirit at last rising in self-defence.   'I will accept it only from Eustace himself.'

'Eustace is far away.   There was some talk of extending his travels to the East. He is resigned at last to the inevitable.'

'He missed me!   He wanted me!' cried poor Kitty.   'Oh, Lady Bellingham, have pity on me!   Only tell me that!   Give me only that tiny grain of comfort in my sorrow, that he missed me a very little.'

'He missed his honour more!'

The cold words had hardly escaped her

lips before she regretted them. Every trace of colour left the face and lips already so pale, yet Kitty braced herself under the blow.

'I have made another terrible mistake,' she said, in a voice out of which all tone had departed. 'Perhaps, since I have been away, I have dwelt too much on his kindness to me, on what I thought his affection. I did not think that this would have destroyed it. Perhaps'—her voice was so low that Lady Bellingham could hardly catch the words—'perhaps I ought to thank you for undeceiving me and putting me on a right footing. I will do what is right. When Eustace comes home, I will write to him, and abide by his decision.'

With a strong effort she stood upright, put on her hat, and wound the white gauze veil round her throat.

Lady Bellingham rose; she was frightened at what she had done; her voice shook.

' What do you want me to do?' she said.

' Let me pass,' answered Kitty quietly. She left the room, and went swiftly downstairs. She was in the street before she had given one thought to what she was to do next. The streets were crowded with people, all coming out to breathe the cooler air after the heat of the day. Kitty threaded her way through them mechanically. She knew that there were other trains that would take her back to Santa Chiara that night. Her one idea was to go at once— to leave this terrible Florence far behind.

She was nearly fainting, between exhaustion and misery, before she arrived at the station. She found that she had several hours to wait—long hours in that dreary waiting-room. She tried to eat in the restaurant, but she could not swallow; the neuralgia in her throat, which she had scarcely felt since she had found comparative rest at Santa Chiara, seized upon her again with its iron hand.

At last she found herself safely within the railway carriage, and alone. There had come upon her a sense of utter loneliness, of complete desolation, such as she had never experienced before. It was overwhelming. She thought of the tender, almost superfluous, care that her husband had always lavished on her; of his protection, his constant thought for her; and, in bitter contrast, the drifting about of her present life. It was fortunate that she was alone, for the long pent-up agony broke into a storm of sobs and tears; and, as she rocked herself backwards and forwards, the cry burst from her lips:

'My punishment is greater than I can bear!'

CHAPTER XIII.

DR. MENELLO came into Palazzo St. Isidoro about twelve o'clock, and asked for the Priore. He was taken into the dining-room, where Don Paolo and his mother were just about to breakfast.

'Will you give me some food?' he said. 'I shall not have time to go home, and I want to talk to you.'

Marie's answer was to put before him all that he could possibly need.

'You must not neglect eating,' she said ;

'that is the way you busy people play with your health. A doctor should know better.'

He was very much at home with them now, and he laughed and did full justice to the fare which was set before him.

'I think that when one is very strong, it is difficult to believe that one can ever be otherwise,' said Don Paolo. 'I, thank God, have never known illness.'

'Nor I,' answered Menello. 'It is the best gift of all. In the hospitals they used to look on me as something almost super-natural. Most of the students go through some, at least, of the infectious illnesses.'

'I wonder,' said Don Paolo thoughtfully, 'whether we who are always strong can enter fully into the sufferings of others.'

'I look upon imagination as more power-ful than experience,' said Menello.

'Perhaps so ; but it may be as defective

as the effect of colour on the colour-blind. Who knows?'

'Well,' said Menello, 'we cannot hope to be exempt from the common doom; we shall know some day.'

'Please God,' said Don Paolo.

'You desire it?' cried Marie, shrinking involuntarily.

Don Paolo answered softly, 'The way of the Cross,' and there was a moment's silence. Menello broke it. He had pushed back his chair and risen from table.

'I do not know whether you always confide in madame your mother,' he said. 'May I speak freely before her?'

'Yes, yes; we have no concealments in these times,' said Don Paolo hastily. 'It has begun, then? I thought so, from your manner.'

'What has begun?' cried Marie. 'What are you saying?'

'It is only what we have been expecting and preparing for,' said Menello. 'The cholera has come.'

'Ah! God in His mercy help us!'

'Where is it, and in what streets?'

'Three cases already,' answered the doctor; 'two in one family, the Lucis; another in the Borgo Alessandro.'

'Who there?'

'Mattei; he is dead. The other cases are in Bruni's hands. He was unwilling to believe it at first, but I looked in as I passed the house this morning. Bruni came out to tell me there was no doubt at all; the symptoms were Asiatic, and of a virulent type. Now, my friend, if you can come, there are preparations at the hospital to make at once. I want you to manage the authorities for me. I wish we were more ready,' he went on, with a look of care; 'but it is so hard to move these slow officials. The disinfectants I sent for have not even arrived.'

Don Paolo was quite ready. Marie stood up to bid them farewell. She was very pale. Menello looked at her earnestly.

'Will you forgive me for asking you, signora?' he said; 'but are you nervous about infection?'

'By nature I am very nervous,' answered Marie, smiling with an effort. 'But I am well used to conquering it, and I hope I shall soon get used to it now.'

'Try hard,' said Menello gravely. 'It will be most valuable to us all by-and-by.' He added suddenly: 'The little white lady, your friend, is looking so ill.'

'But she is in Florence!'

'Pardon—she has returned. I am afraid she has had bad news. But I must not linger,' and he hastily followed Don Paolo downstairs.

Madame de St. Isidoro was startled. Kitty had returned. It seemed impossible that her effort for reconciliation should have been rejected. She could not bear to think so.

It was the full heat of the day, when everyone was lying on their beds with closed persiennes, and as much ice as they could afford in the room. But Marie could not wait ; she went downstairs, hardly stopping to throw a lace veil over her head and open a great white umbrella as she hurried off to the Casa Rossa.

She found Kitty lying down, worn out and exhausted by crying, so unhinged that her friend remained with her all day, feeling that she could be of more use looking after her than at home. Towards evening the exhaustion changed into painful restlessness —she paced up and down the rooms, sat down for a few moments, and then resumed her walk.

Lady Bellingham's reception of her had given her a shock from which she could not recover. It was a revelation to her; and as she had more time in which to think it over, the more convinced she became that her mother-in-law was right, that the wrong she had done in leaving her husband could not be so easily condoned.

Marie did not know how to comfort her; and she longed desperately for five minutes of her son. He would know what to say. It seemed to her a skein too much tangled ever to be unravelled; and she did not know what line it would be safest and wisest to take—whether to preach patience and perseverance, or resignation to the inevitable.

After all, the tender soothing and caressing she gave to her poor little heart-broken friend was as good for her as any advice; and of this tender soothing Marie di St. Isidoro was a very mistress—the very touch of her hand and sound of her voice carrying with them a comforting power.

It was growing late in the afternoon, and Madame di St. Isidoro began to think of returning home.

'I wish I could persuade you to come home with me, Kitty,' she said. 'I cannot bear to leave you here in this loneliness.'

'I almost think that I must,' said Kitty, holding her hand fast. 'I am afraid that, after all, I am not brave enough to live alone.'

'Poor child! You have overrated your own strength,' said Marie. 'Well, will you come to-night, or wait till to-morrow?'

'To-morrow—I must not offend the good Palmettos. Are you sure you will not mind? Shall I not be in the Priore's way?'

'He will welcome you——' she began, but before she had finished the sentence she was interrupted by the entrance of Signora Palmetto, the landlady of the Casa Rossa.

She was a little, dark, stout woman, with quick black eyes and an ever-gleaming smile ; but this evening the plump face seemed to have fallen into strange lines, and her voice was strained and querulous. She had two children—a boy and a girl—and those children were the idols. of their parents.

'What is it, Signora Padrona?' said Kitty, at the sight of her face. 'Surely something must have gone wrong?'

'Santa Madonna! Wrong? I should think things have gone wrong! Why, they say the cholera is come! But it cannot be true; it must be mere gossip. Is it not so, dear Signora Marchesa?' and she looked at Marie, wringing her small fat hands.

'And if the cholera did come, that is no

reason why it should attack you,' said Marie consolingly. 'Alas! it is the poor, who are half starved, who suffer most.'

'Then it is true?'

'It is true that there have been one or two cases in the town.'

'Ah, then we shall go at once; we can never stay here. Beppo would never allow it. Oh, la! la! what will become of us all?'

Kitty was standing quite still—a bright flush upon her cheek.

'Signora Palmetto,' she exclaimed, 'tell me what you have heard!'

'Heard? Enough to terrify any woman. The Lucis, in the Borgo Alessandro, have two children ill; and Dr. Bruni has never left them. And now Nino has just come in crying like a child, asking me for blankets, and I don't know what else. He says Assunta is taken ill!'

'Assunta?　With all those little children and an infant !　What will become of them ?'

'He was shaking from head to foot.　"It is the cholera!" he said.　"It can be nothing else."　They say the Luci children will not live.　Assunta was in the torture of Purgatory.　Blankets !　I gave him one for the love of heaven—but it shall never come back to this house again ;　no, no! And to-morrow Beppo must make up his mind to go, for I leave the town, and I will not stir without him.　If only we could persuade you to come with us, dear signora.　We have a little villa in the hills of the Mugello—it is far from danger ;　one can get eggs and fowls there.'

But Kitty had risen to her feet, and was quietly fastening on her hat.

'Are you going out ?' said Marie wonderingly.　'Are you not too tired ?'

'I am going to see what I can do for poor Assunta,' answered Kitty.

The padrona gave a little shriek.

'But it is madness! madness!' she cried.

Marie spoke very calmly.

'Dear Kitty, have you considered well? You know that this is only the beginning : it will be very bad ! Do you mean to make it your work ?'

'It seems so,' said Kitty, with a faint smile. 'It seems as if other ties were cut off on purpose; and my life rendered valueless, perhaps also on purpose.'

'These two ladies have no children,' exclaimed the padrona, shaking with fear and eagerness. 'They cannot appreciate the fears of a mother. If they would only consider——'

Lady Bellingham laid her hand gently on her shoulder; but Signora Palmetto shrank away as if it were already infectious.

'It is not that I want to be unkind, dear signora,' she began, with chattering teeth.

'When I go, I shall not return here,' said Kitty quietly. 'I shall probably find lodgings nearer Borgo Alessandro.'

'No; you will come to me,' said Marie decidedly.

Kitty looked at her earnestly.

'You are not afraid?' she said.

'Afraid? of course I am afraid! We are all terrified; but that is no reason against doing our duty. I shall probably be wanted by-and-by to help; but I shall not volunteer till I am told to do so.'

'My task to-night may be a very simple one,' said Kitty. 'Probably only looking after the baby.'

'And you will not have an idea how to swaddle it, my dear.'

'Then I shall come to you for assistance.'

The padrona stood with open mouth— she could not understand how they could speak gaily at such a moment.

'I go to pack,' she said. 'And you, dear signora, only say what I can do for you. Of course, you would like all your things moved at once? Of course, it will save you much fatigue if you have not to come back here. I will see to it all.'

Kitty could not help smiling at the transparent little ruse. It was settled that her things were to be moved to the Palazzo St. Isidoro, and then the two ladies went out together.

'Good-bye, Marie!' said Kitty, as they crossed the market-place. 'Do not sit up for me. If I can come back I will; but I do not know of what use I may find myself.'

'Good-bye, dearest! God be with you, and preserve you!' answered Marie, as they parted.

Kitty reached Nino's shop. He was a shoemaker on a very small scale. The wife and children lived in rooms above the shop. Charity had made her acquainted before with the family, which was very poor.

The shop was deserted, and Kitty went through it, and upstairs.

The sound of terrible moans made her stop and shudder; but she braced up her courage, and was about to open the door, when Dr. Menello came suddenly out.

'You here!' he exclaimed. 'Signora, have you heard?'

'Yes; I have come to offer my help,' she answered quietly.

'Help? that is well. This case is too far gone for the hospital. I have a Sister here, but the poor children are alone—there is an infant. Not one single neighbour will come near the place, and the Sister cannot leave the woman one moment.'

' I will see to the children.'

'That is right!' he exclaimed heartily.
'And one more thing—will you manage
the disinfectants? These people will not
try. They say it is the will of Heaven!
They will do nothing to save their own
children. You have power over them—
you will exercise it?'

'Only tell me what to do.'

He rapidly gave his instructions; going
away to his other work with a satisfied
feeling that here, at least, his directions
would be carried out.

Kitty found her task no light one. The
poor infant was in a pitiable condition,
from crying and starvation. She sent out
one of the children to buy necessaries; but
to her consternation the child was hunted
back into the house by the panic-stricken
neighbours. But Kitty would not submit;
she went out herself, with the wailing infant

in her arms, and insisted upon having the necessary food and milk supplied to her.

She put the children to bed, and was walking about hushing the baby, whose cries had sunk into little moans, when the Sister came hurriedly out of Assunta's room and called her.

The cholera-cramps were frightful : the only possible relief was given by incessant friction. The Sister's hands were almost paralyzed. Kitty silently took her place. The Sister sat down for a short space, holding the baby, and falling into a sort of rest.

So, through the whole of that night, they relieved each other. With the cold blue of the early dawn Menello came in. The suffering ceased; collapse followed — and death !

Menello stood with a look of deep thought on his face.

'It will be terrible!' he said.

Kitty caught the words as he muttered them to himself. The cholera had begun with such virulence.

The Sister took Lady Bellingham back to the hospital to rest, sending one of the nurses to look after the motherless children.

CHAPTER XIV.

BEFORE many days were over, Santa Chiara was in the midst of one of the most devastating epidemics that had ever visited fair Italy. Everyone fled, who could do so, from the hot streets, on which the sun blazed down day after day with merciless brilliancy. Right and left, in the tall palaces and in the lowest rag-shops and squalid dens alike, the people and the children lay down and died.

Lady Bellingham did not return to the Palazzo St. Isidoro. She remained at the hospital. She was always engaged either there or in nursing cases in their own homes, when it was too late to move the patient, or, as too often happened, there was not one vacant bed.

Kitty seemed to have wonderful strength given to her for her work. She never flagged; she was able to eat well, and to sleep instantly at every spare moment ; and she concentrated her whole mind and thoughts on her duties, her previous sufferings seemingly giving her force and energy. It was a daily, hourly fight with Death.

Kitty made no more effort at concealment. She required constant supplies of money. She wrote her own cheques. She wrote openly to her mother, telling her where she was, and giving her commissions for things wanted at Santa Chiara.

Mrs. Brown-Clifford, after one day of horror at her daughter's proceedings, wisely made the best of it ; did not weary her with remonstrances, but only did as she was told, and did it uncommonly well.

Marie di St. Isidoro did not take part in the nursing. She had neither strength nor nerve for the undertaking ; but she was as useful in her way. She refreshed and fed and encouraged the active workers ; she executed their commissions ; she did all they asked her to do ; she kept her kitchen always at work preparing food for the sick ; and some large rooms were turned into a *crèche* for the children.

For some time the people suffered patiently—lying down to suffer and die with a kind of fatalism against which doctors and nurses fought hard. It was a state of things exceedingly difficult to make head against. The people would take no precautions ; they would not use the disinfectants ; they insisted upon slaking their thirst on the great water-melons they loved; and, though warned again and again, it was of no avail—they would not listen.

But a day arrived on which their resignation gave way. Some mischievous idlers living in the low quarters of the town began to whisper that the cholera came not from the hand of God, but was the result of the vilely smelling stuffs that the doctors insisted upon using in the streets and drains, and in great abundance in infected houses.

Little knots of angry, careworn men got together talking at the corners of the streets, capping each other's stories : how the doctors hung up sheets drenched with strange drugs ; and how, wherever they did so, the patient died ; and there must be something in it.

The more ignorant the people, the more easily were they led. The pain and terror which had at first stupefied, now seemed to madden them till they were ready for anything. Yet, in the midst of it all, at the first symptoms of the dreaded pestilence, hurried frantic messages were sent to fetch the very men they were abusing; and cries of despair arose when doctors and nurses were not forthcoming.

Both doctors and nurses were worked to the utmost. Dr. Bruni was obliged to give up, and leave Santa Chiara for rest; and in his absence Menello took his place as head of the hospital. He was here, there, and everywhere, morning, noon, and night; hardy, strong, and vigorous, with the red line round his eyes of one who has never sufficient sleep. The very sight of him in a sick-room, with his brilliant smile, his never-failing resource and energy, was sufficient to inspire confidence. Yet, strangely enough, it was on him that the discontented vented their spleen. Tender as he was with the suffering, he was stern and indefatigable in enforcing the use of disinfectants; and sometimes enforced his orders by dint of threats of real authority.

The angry feelings became more apparent every day; and they made Don Paolo uneasy. He saw that Menello paid little or no attention to them; and he determined to try and put him on his guard.

The Priore found talking to his people of little use; they listened to him with their habitual deference, but they reserved their own opinion, and never altered it.

One day the Priore stopped Menello coming out of a house in the Strada Reale, and promptly thrust his arm through his.

'Come, Ettore,' he said. 'I will take no denial. Come home to dinner. You have not dined?'

'Not yet, but I will. Only let me run in here for five minutes—this is a hopeful case ; a man from Verona ; I think he will live. That will refresh me ; and I will follow you at once.'

' I shall wait for you outside. You will remember that I am waiting, and not be long.'

Menello nodded, and disappeared up the enormously tall flight of stone stairs, on the topmost flight of which lived his patient.

Five minutes after, an upper window opened. Menello beckoned, and the Priore went in.

When they re-emerged half an hour later, Menello was very pale, and he brushed away the drops from his brow with a strange look of depression.

' Well, my friend ?'

' I was wrong, you see,' said the young doctor slowly. ' I hoped—and he is dead. We must be reaching a crisis, now—no one gets well. We are helpless in the hands of God! Medicines fail! Skill and science go for nothing! What remains?'

The burst of despondency startled Don Paolo.

'We must pray, pray hard that the plague may be stayed,' he said earnestly.

'Yes, pray, pray,' answered Menello, 'for it has become a frightful thing. Oh for rain! for sweet fresh water and clouds over that terrible blue sky, and a good blast of fresh strong wind!'

He breathed hard, almost gasping, but the air was heavy and hot, and the close, sickening smell hung like a vapour over the streets.

Menello shook himself.

'Come, come,' he said, 'I must not behave like that. Have you any champagne, Priore? I am afraid of wine just now; but, as it happens, I have not been in bed all night, and I missed my turn of sleep at the hospital yesterday. So give me some food, a glass of champagne, and an hour's quiet, and you will be doing good service.'

They found Marie and Kitty both in the house. Kitty wanted to speak to Don Paolo, and had come for the purpose. When she saw Menello she began to speak to him at once on business, but the Priore stopped her.

'Not now, Lady Bellingham,' he said; 'let him eat and sleep.'

'You did not sleep, then, last night?'

'No.'

Kitty and Marie went away to another room. The Priore took Menello upstairs, and did not quit him till he saw him throw himself on his own bed, and instantly, without a moment's pause, fall into profound sleep. Then he came down to Kitty.

She wanted to say a very few words to

him, but she could hardly spare the time, as her duty would take her back to the hospital at once.

'You wished to see me?' he said kindly. 'You know how willingly I would do anything in my power for you, and not only for you, but for your husband. There are few men whom I know so slightly in whom I take so great an interest.'

Kitty's eyes filled with tears.

'It is about him I would speak to you,' she said, pressing her hands nervously together. 'Marie has told you what happened to me at Florence?'

'Yes, but your mother-in-law's view is not necessarily that of your husband.'

'Perhaps not,' said poor Kitty, controlling herself with some difficulty. 'But this is what I want to say. You know how precarious life is just now.'

The Priore nodded.

'Any moment I may be taken away. I have written to Eustace. I want you, in case anything should happen to me, to send him the letter, with some words from yourself. You have so great a gift of persuasion, you could make him forgive me, and perhaps grant me a little love in memory of the past.'

'I will do as you wish. Just now it would not be right for me to leave Santa Chiara; there is the infection to be thought of, and the work here. Were it otherwise, I would go and seek him for you.'

'No, no; now is not the time. He is not in Italy; he may be very far away.'

'No, we must wait; but do not lose heart. I am very hopeful that all will go well. He and you have both much to forgive and much to forget. Do not be afraid. God will bring it to pass.'

'Then I may leave the letter with you?'

'Yes; it shall be as you wish.'

He was still speaking when Marie came in hastily.

'A very urgent message has come for Dr. Menello,' she said. 'What shall we do?'

'He must sometimes rest,' said Don Paolo. 'A man cannot live the life he is living long.'

'I will go,' said Kitty. 'If I find that his presence is indispensable I will send you a message.'

'You are not overtired?'

'Oh no; I had a long night's rest last night.'

Kitty's face had on it a look so wistful, so pathetic, that Marie could not help stealing her arm round her, and kissing her yearningly.

'Can nothing be done?' she said to her son, after she had left them. 'She is very strong, and wonderfully brave ; but I think her heart is breaking, poor child!'

'I shall write to her husband,' said Don Paolo quietly. 'He ought to know. His mother is a woman for whom I have but very little respect. She had no right to act as she has done—no right whatever.'

It was not often that he spoke like that. Marie saw that he was strongly moved, and she said no more ; only nodded quietly, and went about some of the numerous works of mercy that fell to her share.

Don Paolo sat down and wrote his letter ; a simple one, but long and full of detail. He began by telling Sir Eustace the whole story of the life his brave little wife was now leading. He allowed the facts to speak for themselves, making no comment on the calm, reliable usefulness she shared. He then went on to ask whether the reception she had met with from her mother-in-law was the same that she might expect from himself; and he finished with a few short words in his character as priest, pointing out that first and foremost in the battle of life stood out duty, distinct, uncompromising, but a *sine quâ non* on the road to salvation.

He directed the letter to Castleford, to be forwarded, thinking that it would be more likely by that means to reach its destination.

Presently Menello came in, bright, erect, and rested.

'No message for me?' he asked.

The Priore told him what had happened, and he nodded.

'The little white lady knows all that there is to do,' he said. 'My patients are always safe in her hands. I will follow her. What a crowd there is in the street!' he exclaimed suddenly, as he perceived through the persiennes an unusual gathering below. 'Well, I must begone. *Au revoir*, dear madame.'

And with his usual quick alert tread he ran downstairs.

Don Paolo was slowly sealing his letter, wondering whether he had said enough, when quite suddenly a roar arose from the street below, which made him leap to his feet and tear open the persiennes.

At the sight of Menello on the door-step a great shout had risen.

'Here he is!—the assassin! the murderer! the man who poisons us, and calls it cholera!'

Men and women gathered furiously round him, menacing him with looks and gestures. Don Paolo could see that he was keeping his temper perfectly well; he fancied that he could hear his voice in cheery, conciliatory tones. But the fast gathering mob was not to be appeased; some ringleaders among them seemed to be urging them on; they were pressing upon him more and more. For a moment he all but lost his footing, but recovered with a strong effort. The din and uproar grew greater. At last the Priore, from his window, perceived, to his horror, that Menello was actually fighting for his life.

He paused not for a single moment, but dashed downstairs. He was a powerful, well-knit man. He forced his way through the mob of struggling men and shrieking women, dashing them right and left, till he reached his friend. Menello's teeth were fast clenched, his coat was torn to atoms. He had now a dangerous look on his face. His strength, tried as it was by constant over-exertion, was twice that of any two of the miserably sickly crowd of men who were attacking him.

' Ettore !' shouted Don Paolo ; and he glanced back, crying :

' Go back, go back, Priore!   This is no scene for you !'

At this moment his head was violently jerked backwards by a virago who was tearing at his hair.   He could not strike her; he could only thrust her aside, and, by doing so, gain the wall and plant himself with his back to it; but his face was getting more and more dangerous.

Don Paolo forced his way to him.   The people fell back, both from respect to him and from the sweep of his powerful arm.

' Cowards!   Ungrateful!' he exclaimed, and the sound of his voice, so familiar to their ears, held them in momentary check. ' Fiends!   To attack a man who is giving his life to save yours !'

' The poison! the poison!' they shouted.

' Poison! There is but one poison, the deadly infection of the cholera. He is engaged in fighting it night and day. You will not have it? So be it. Let him go free with me, and the next victim shall die without his aid.'

A perfect yell of rage followed his words.

' If we must die, let us die like Christians, not like poisoned vermin!' shouted a voice.

' Why, Ponti!' cried the Priore. ' You, of all people! The *Signor Dottore* sat up with your children three nights running, and I heard that he had saved them all.'

' Yes, yes!' cried the man. ' But not till I had torn down the poison-sheet over the door.'

' The consequence of which was that the others in the same house caught the infection.'

'And that is true!' cried a pale, thin man, with a shrill, piping voice. 'And not till you did that did my little Peppina sicken; and she did not live. She died! she died!'

His voice rose to a shrill kind of wail.

The mob stopped their violent surging to and fro, and Menello, with a vigorous movement, shook himself free. The haggard man thrust himself forward, shrieking :

'I will tell the truth—the truth! The doctor did all he could to save her, and when she went I tore down the poison-sheet, and said, " If Peppina is dead, what does it matter to me who dies also?" '

'He takes the bread out of the hands of the poor!' shouted the old vendor of water-melons. ' He brought down the law upon us when we were already starving for want of something to drink.'

At that moment a frightful cry rang through the crowd, and a man with wild eyes and tattered clothes hurled himself through them, gasping, panting, clinging from one side to another, to rebound like a wild cat.

'*Dottore! dottore! Signor Dottore!* Where is Menello? Come at once. It has come to us at last. I swore to the Blessed Madonna that it should not come to us, but it has come. Serafina is ill; she is in torture; she dies! Heart of stone! why are you so slow?'

He had reached Menello, and clung to him, his grasping, claw-like hands catching at his breast.

Menello shook him off.

'Why should I come to you?' he said roughly. 'Let the people die. I have done with them.'

A shout rose from the mob, a kind of

howl or wail. Menello looked round him fiercely.

'Am I a saint?' he exclaimed. 'Am I more than man, that you expect me hourly to risk my life for such a reward as this?'

And he held up his arms, from which the torn strips of his coat were hanging, and the tattered shirt-sleeves, blood-stained from bleeding wrists and knuckles.

The Priore stood watching the scene. He knew the man well, and had no fear as to his ultimate action.

The changeable crowd broke into sobs and wails. The unfortunate suppliant renewed his passionate cry:

'I have done nothing—nothing!' he cried. 'And Serafina is dying, and what is to become of the children? And it is torture —the torture is horrible. For the love of Heaven, *Signor Dottore*—for the love of your own mother, do not waste the precious time! Hearts of stone!' he cried, turning with a fierce snarl upon the crowd, ' this is your doing! And Serafina dies—dies—she dies!'

'I will not go!' cried Menello passionately.

Then the Priore looked up, an anxious light in his eyes. The crowd pressed close now; some went down on their knees. They implored forgiveness; they promised anything and everything if he would yield. A kind of despair had come over them. What was to happen if they could get no succour at all? The reaction was as powerful as the tumult itself had been.

Menello stood quite still; then, with a violent effort, he seemed to master himself, and he spoke in his usual voice:

' Come, come; if, after all, you cannot do without your poisoner, let me get through.'

They gathered round him, praising, thanking, trying to kiss his hands. Their demonstrations were intensely irritating to a man who had just been actually struggling for life among them ; but he could not get rid of them till he reached the actual door where the woman lay dying, and there at last they dispersed, leaving him to the usual hand-to-hand fight with Agony and Death, to which he was so accustomed night and day.

The Priore did not wait to see the end. When he saw Menello yield, he returned to his own work with a smile on his face and a thanksgiving in his heart.

CHAPTER XV.

ADY BELLINGHAM sat in her large, cool, comfortable salon at the Hotel dell' Arno, but she herself was neither comfortable nor cool; in fact, she was in a very excited state of mind. She wrote a note with a hasty hand, rang the bell sharply, and desired her maid to send it off, and then to return to her. After which she threw herself back in her chair and fanned herself violently.

'If you have frightened me like this for nothing, Johnson!' she exclaimed when her maid came back, 'I shall not forgive you easily.'

' It is not for nothing, my lady,' answered the maid glibly. ' I only repeated what all the world is saying ; there is never an evening that we sit down to dinner without fresh stories and fresh reports.'

' Why did you never tell me before ?' she said sharply.

Johnson hesitated. The truth was that she had been very happy and enjoyed herself greatly at the Hotel dell' Arno in the company of an attractive Italian lady's-maid and courier, and she had done her best to keep all cholera reports from her mistress ; but the Italian servants were gone. They had been seized with panic on their own account, and had succeeded in alarming and dislodging their family, and Johnson wanted to go also.

' Why should I alarm you for nothing, my lady ?' she said.

' If there is quarantine now established

on all the railways, we are already too late.
It is insufferable !   Your conduct has been
very bad !'

Johnson looked sullen.

' What more have you heard now ?' said
Lady Bellingham, still fanning herself
rapidly.

' Nothing particularly new, my lady. The
cholera is raging at Santa Chiara, the deaths
from 150 a day ; and there has been a riot
there because the doctors will use disinfectants.'

' At Santa Chiara !' exclaimed Lady Bellingham.

It gave her a shock she could not quite
conceal. She herself had driven back her
daughter-in-law into the very midst of the
danger.

' It is particularly violent there, my lady,'
went on the maid. ' You may remember
how I used to point out to your ladyship

what a crowded, unhealthy kind of place it was—very different from Florence.'

' But the quarantine ?'

' They shut up all the people who arrive in trains in a lazaretto, and keep them three weeks.'

' Three weeks !' cried Lady Bellingham.

' Yes, three weeks, my lady. I heard it with my own ears ; and the lazarettos are not at all commodious. You have to herd together as you can—three, four, and five in a room—and just eat what they choose to fling at you. This is what has come of staying in foreign parts !'

' I don't believe it !' exclaimed Lady Bellingham.

' There is another way, my lady. In some places they put you all together—fifty, sixty, or a hundred—in a small room, and shut up every chink, and then blow in upon you some kind of gas, which smells fearfully; and you choke, and struggle, and scream, and fight, but they only laugh outside. One maid told me she knew another maid, whose lady had died of it. The gas went into her head, and she had a fit and never came round again. I don't know which is the best of the two.'

' Almost worse than the cholera itself!'

' But, my lady, how can you tell when you are in the lazaretto whether the person sleeping in your very room will not have the cholera the next moment? For the whole object of shutting you up is that you may all have it together.'

Lady Bellingham stamped her foot.

' Go, Johnson!' she exclaimed. ' Do you want to terrify me, now that I have not got Miss Bellingham to help me? Let me not hear one word more about it.'

' And I am not to pack, my lady?'

' I will let you know later. Lord Austen

will come and talk to me, then I will settle.'

The maid went away.

Lady Bellingham was frightened out of her wits. All the alternatives suggested by her maid were dreadful to her. She sat on thorns until the time came when she thought she might expect an answer to her note.

Marion came herself. She looked exceedingly beautiful as she came forward to kiss her friend.

'Austen is out, I am sorry to say,' she said; 'but as " Immediate " was on your note, I opened it, and came to see if I could do anything for you. You do not look well.'

'I am quite well, my dear May. What nonsense! Nothing of the sort!' and she rose hastily, and looked at herself in a mirror. 'I am not at all pale or flushed. It is not about my health.'

Marion seated herself.

‘I thought something must have troubled you,’ she said, in her calm, sweet voice. ‘Austen will be home this evening ; he has gone to Pisa to see a friend of his who is there—an Italian painter. It was an old promise, or he would not have gone in such weather as this.’

‘He ought not to go ; travelling is not safe. It is about that I want to ask his advice. I want to get home at once, and I don’t know how to manage it.’

‘Is it on account of the cholera?’

‘I think even more on account of the quarantine. People like ourselves, who live well, and in healthy houses, and under medical advice, don’t have cholera.’

‘Did you see the account of Santa Chiara?’ said Marion gravely.

‘No ; I hardly touch the papers now— they smell so horribly of carbolic acid.

Johnson tells me that they are all fumigated, and it makes me so terribly nervous.'

'You have friends at Santa Chiara ?'

'Yes; but do not speak of them—one cannot bear to think of people one knows in such a position.'

'It must be terrible,' said Marion. 'I saw something of cholera once, many years ago, when I was a child. This at Santa Chiara is one of the worst outbreaks in Italy.'

'My dear Marion,' said Lady Bellingham fretfully, 'can't you see how nervous I am, and talk of something else ? Is it true that there is quarantine on all the Italian lines ?'

'No,' answered Marion; 'the Riviera is still open. I suppose we shall be leaving soon; shall we arrange to go together ?'

'In the middle of your honeymoon, my dear !'

'Never mind that,' said Marion; 'only I don't think Austen will be ready to go quite yet. I will talk to him about it.'

'I cannot wait; I must go at once.'

Marion saw that a sort of panic was taking possession of her friend: her hands and head were trembling.

'Dear Lady Bellingham,' she said, 'do not be so nervous. There have been no signs of cholera at Florence—not a rumour even; and Santa Chiara is at least six hours off.'

'They say that one lady was killed by the fumigation!' exclaimed Lady Bellingham.

'Oh, but they talk great nonsense! I have been through it myself, and they always make up the same story of the lady being killed. It is extremely disagreeable, but I am quite sure it never killed anybody.'

As she was speaking, a waiter brought in a telegram for Lady Bellingham.

'Take it, Marion,' she said faintly. 'Open it, and let me know the worst at once.'

A horrible misgiving had come over her that it brought bad news from Santa Chiara—that Kitty must be ill, perhaps dead. Kitty was always present to her mind now—a painful weight on her conscience.

Marion opened the telegram.

'It is all right,' she said cheerily; 'nothing in the least alarming. It is from Eustace. The yacht is at Civita Vecchia. They will be here early to-morrow morning.'

'What on earth is he coming here for?' cried Lady Bellingham, speaking snappishly in her relief. 'I thought that he was going to the East.'

'This is what he says'—and she read aloud :

'" Shall be with you to-morrow, six o'clock, with Alice, ready to take you home. — On board the *Seagull*, Civita Vecchia."'

' Well, I suppose he has some good reason for changing his plans.'

' Perhaps there may be news of Kitty. Ah! that indeed would be happiness!'

' Not at all likely. How could they have news of Kitty out at sea? Why, they must have been at least three weeks already at Civita Vecchia, if it is true that the Mediterranean ports are closed.'

' It depends on where they come from,' said Marion.

' Nonsense, my dear! It means that, whether they go in or out, or wherever they come from or go to, they have to lie rocking about outside in the open sea in all the harbour dirt and smells.'

Marion did not attempt to correct the idea.

'You will be all right now,' she said. 'Eustace will take care of you, and take you home. You must have missed Alice dreadfully.'

'I only hope Alice will come back in a more cheerful frame of mind.'

'Ah! if only this return might mean news of Kitty!'

Lady Bellingham made no answer. A misgiving had come across her that perhaps they *had* heard of Kitty—perhaps knew that she was at Santa Chiara. If so, whatever happened, Eustace must be prevented going there.

'I will not let Eustace go to Santa Chiara!' she exclaimed, quite suddenly—so suddenly that Marion was startled.

'No, of course not; why should he go there? What should attract him? It would not be at all prudent. Surely you do not mean——'

'Nothing,' interrupted Lady Bellingham. 'Only he is so obstinate. There are people there with whom he formed the most romantic, unheard-of friendship. You have heard of Ursel?'

'Ursel?—of course. Is he there?'

'It is his home. And Don Paolo St. Isidoro—Eustace thinks nobody equal to him.'

'Ah, yes—the great mission preacher. I knew him also in old days. He was very good to my mother. I forgot for the moment that he was there.'

'Eustace shall not go; you will help to prevent it?'

'He is not likely to wish it,' said Marion gently. 'Why should he? He would be of no use to them.'

'He is so headstrong and perverse.'

Marion made no answer. She could not endure to hear his mother speak of him like this.

'Well,' she said, rising, 'as I can do nothing for you now, Lady Bellingham, I will go. Eustace will be able to take you home quite comfortably. You see, he can have no idea of going to Santa Chiara. He expressly says in his telegram that he is ready to take you home. Good-bye. Austen may perhaps look in on you this 'evening ; and, meanwhile, you might let your maid begin to pack.'

'I will, without a moment's delay.'

Marion returned home. Lady Bellingham was left to her own unpleasant reflections. Suddenly she rang for her maid.

'Bring me all the letters that have arrived for Sir Eustace,' she said. And a large bundle forwarded from Castleford was brought to her.

Lady Bellingham studied them all carefully, turning them round and round with dainty fingers. There appeared nothing to cause her misgivings; and she tied them up again.

Suddenly her maid returned.

'Pardon, my lady, but this little thin letter tumbled out—I found it on the floor. Pah! How it smells!'

Lady Bellingham took it up eagerly, in spite of the strong odour of carbolic acid, and the maid left her.

Lady Bellingham saw the Santa Chiara postmark, and flung it down as if it were a stinging insect! As she looked at it lying at her feet, she grew excessively pale. The handwriting was not Kitty's; neither was it Marie's. It was altogether strange to her. The terror of what that letter might contain was so great that she could not face it. She hastily opened a flacon of aromatic vinegar; poured it over her own hands and the letter, and tore it open.

It was the Priore's letter to her son. She

read it through, her brow growing scarlet with impatience and anger that this man should presume to rebuke her son.

Then a cold chill followed upon her anger. What would Eustace say if it ever came to his knowledge that she had repulsed his wife?

In that moment a horrible temptation came over her to wish that Kitty would lose her life among the miserable sufferers for whom she was working; and then the Gordian knot would be cut, and he would never know.

Lady Bellingham had become aware that that day's action had been the worst mistake of her life.

She deliberately tore up the letter into a thousand tiny pieces; and, not content with that, lit a match and consumed them all with elaborate care.

CHAPTER XVI.

LADY BELLINGHAM sent a note of farewell to the Austens' villa, saying that she had made up her mind to go at once.

She kept her maid up all night packing. Her longing to quit Florence had become a perfect panic. She discovered that an available train left for Genoa at 9.40 ; and she ordered warm baths and breakfasts for her son and daughter to be ready, so that they might refresh themselves with all possible speed, and be ready to start again at once.

Lady Bellingham was up and dressed ready to receive the travellers when they arrived the next morning, to their very great surprise.

'Why, mother, is the world coming to an end?' were Eustace's first words. 'Fancy you being up at this hour in the morning! and you look tired already.'

' There is so little time to lose,' said Lady Bellingham. ' Everything is ready for you —hot water and all ; for the train starts at 9.40.'

' I don't think Alice ought to go on at once, mother,' said Eustace quickly. ' We have had a very hot and tiring journey. She will be quite worn out.'

' Oh, that can't be helped. There is no time to lose. Any day they may put on quarantine! My one idea is to get you both out of this horrible Italy!'

They saw how it was; and Alice stopped her brother's expostulations.

'I can manage perfectly well, Eu,' she said. 'Only wait till after breakfast—you will see how wonderfully refreshed we shall be.'

Lady Bellingham, in her excited frame of mind, had expected to see them arrive with bright faces, full of eagerness over their travels. She was intensely irritated by the disappointment. The look of care and anxiety had deepened, rather than diminished, on her son's face ; his smiles were rare and very grave ; he was so thin as to be almost haggard ; and his eyes were restless.

Alice looked very tired—so tired that, at a calmer moment, her mother would not even have dreamt of making her continue her journey. The consciousness of this increased Lady Bellingham's impatience.

Eustace followed his sister to the room prepared for her, saying tenderly :

'Alice dear, can you manage it? If not, I am sure you could stay here for a few days with May; and I would come back and fetch you.'

'On no account!' exclaimed Alice eagerly. 'I can go on perfectly. I am only glad to get back to mamma, for she is evidently in a most nervous state.'

Eustace went away. He and Alice had returned to all their old charming intercourse with each other, and it had comforted and helped both of them greatly.

Lady Bellingham would willingly have hurried them over their breakfast, but Eustace would not allow that; there was really plenty of time. At last his presence and undertaking of all the arrangements had a soothing effect on his mother, and she had time to ask them what had changed their plans and brought them to Florence.

The reasons were several.

Georgie, for the first time in her life, had suffered severely from sea-sickness; the slow swell of an unusually calm sea had proved too much for even her, and she wished to land to recover herself. Then came the cholera reports — getting daily worse and worse—and rumours of the exceeding discomfort of quarantine. Eustace determined to go to Florence, and take his mother home at once. The Mulroys would stay at Civita Vecchia awhile, and he would rejoin them later, wherever the yacht might be.

At nine o'clock Lady Bellingham would no longer be deterred from starting for the station. The bills were paid; and, in spite of the forty minutes to spare, to which Eustace gave a little impatient sigh, they departed.

The post came in early at Florence, and about nine o'clock that morning a letter was placed in Lady Austen's hands, which caused her to leap up from the breakfast-table with a little cry:

' Oh, Austen, Austen!—a letter in Kitty's handwriting!'

She tore it open.

Lord Austen was little less eager than herself.

' At last!' he exclaimed. ' Please God it contain good news!'

Marion was reading it through, the colour coming and going rapidly in her cheeks. She put it down with a kind of gasp.

'I cannot understand it!' she exclaimed. ' She has been here; what can have happened? Read it, Austen—read it aloud, that I may take it in better.'

He took it up, and read:

' My dear Lady Austen,

' Will you forgive me for troubling you with this letter and the many requests

it contains? but I cannot do otherwise. If
I had known that you were at Florence
when I went there, I think I must have
gone to ask you to see me; but I am glad
now that I did not, for I think that if you
also had rejected me, it would have been
more than I could have borne. I did all I
have done from what I thought unselfish
motives. Don Paolo has shown me that I
was wrong; so now I am a suppliant, not
for reconciliation so much as for forgiveness. Some day, perhaps, that may come.

'I must not take up your time with my
affairs. I saw in the paper that you were
at Florence. We are, you know, in the
midst of a terrible outbreak of cholera, and
I am helping in the hospital. We are short
of nurses, for the pressure of work is very
great. I am in want of a great many
things, and you do not know how grateful
I shall be to you if you would send them

to me at once with the smallest possible
delay. We want linen, and good wine, and
arrowroot, and flannel, and as much cam-
phor as you can find in the shops; and I
cannot get good smelling-salts here.

' If you can send me these things, I shall be
thankful. My mother sends supplies from
England; but they come so slowly. I
enclose a list of quantities. You see, my
demand is not a trifling one; only, if you
can, please lose no time.

' Dear Marion, I shall never forget your
kindness to me!

' Your affectionate

' KITTY.'

' I wonder whether Eustace has arrived!'
exclaimed Lord Austen; and again Marion
started from her chair.

' Arrived! I am afraid both arrived and
started again. The nine-forty train—oh!
is there time?'

'I hope so. There may be. It is a quarter-past now. I will make all the haste I can.'

' Bring him here if you can. All depends on his action now.'

Austen was gone before she had finished speaking.

Meanwhile Lady Bellingham had arrived at the station, and by dint of bribery of the officials had been allowed to take her place in the train. Then, and not till then, did she begin to feel some sense of security and comfort again.

Eustace would not get in — he was cramped from travelling all night. He looked forward to another eighteen hours of travelling in the blazing heat with much dismay. He walked up and down the platform smoking, determined to do so to the last moment.

He looked at his watch—two minutes

more remained. The guard unlocked the waiting-rooms, and the passengers rushed out. Secure in the possession of a coupé, still he did not get in; when suddenly he felt a hand on his shoulder, and a hearty English voice exclaiming :

'Just in time—only just! My dear fellow, I never was so pleased to see any-one in my life. Make your mother get out —she cannot go! Make haste, I say! Lady Bellingham, will you kindly get out? I have brought your son news of his wife. You cannot start to-day.'

There was no time for a word of re-monstrance—the two men in front, Alice urging behind, the guard shouting 'Partenza!' and banging all the open doors of the carriages as he passed up the line. She was out with her dressing-case and bag, and had only time to see the agonized expression on the face of her maid as she was borne away in solitary glory in the departing train.

Lady Bellingham sank down on the nearest bench with a look of despair. Alice attended to her while trying to watch her brother, whose face had become so white as to be almost ghastly.

'It is all right,' said Lord Austen; 'May heard from your wife this morning. She is quite well—she is at Santa Chiara.'

'Santa Chiara!'

Lord Austen had not thought of the deadly danger; the sharp shudder Eustace gave when he heard it enlightened him.

'Do not let us stay here,' he said quickly. 'Marion wants to see you. Come back with me at once. I am sorry to have been the means of interrupting your journey,' he said to Lady Bellingham, trying very hard to be polite; 'but we cannot regret it—can we?'

They called a cab, put Lady Bellingham and Alice into it, and saw them drive off to the hotel; then they also took a carriage.

'Tell me what you can, Austen,' said Eustace, with dry lips.

Lord Austen put Kitty's letter into his hands.

At the first part of its contents his amazement was keen.

'What can it mean?' he exclaimed. 'Rejection! What can have happened?'

When he came to all the commissions, he could hardly be restrained from starting off to fulfil them at once.

They reached the Austens' villa, and Lord Austen left Eustace while he went to find Marion.

She was waiting in a fever of anxiety. When she saw him she ran forward, exclaiming:

'Were you in time?'

'Only just in time,' he answered. 'I almost wish you could have seen the face of the old harridan, Bellingham, when we literally tore her out of the train.'

'Poor Lady Bellingham!' said Marion, laughing nervously.

'And now,' said Austen, suddenly stooping and looking into his wife's face, 'what is the next move?'

'Whatever you think best.'

'This is what I think best,' he said, putting his arm round her. 'You had better see him at once, find out his real feeling about his poor, unhappy little wife, and perhaps do what you can do better than anyone living—effect a reconciliation between them.'

'I will do whatever you wish,' she said, clinging to him.

The very closeness of that clinging, the pressure of her lovely head on his shoulder, gave him a sudden little thrill of fear. Why did she hold him so fast? Was she afraid of herself ? Was the recollection of the last time they had met too much for her?

He moved a little away from her, and said, in a voice that had suddenly grown changed and hoarse :

' Do not do it if you would rather not, May.'

She looked up at him, her large, soft eyes full of tears.

' But I would like to try,' she said. ' It may be the fulfilment of one of the greatest hopes of my life, that he should at last be as happy as I am.'

'My darling ! my darling ! you are happy ?' he exclaimed passionately.

She answered very softly :

' So happy, that all my prayers are thanksgivings. Has not God given me the greatest happiness on earth ?'

He had reaped the full reward of long years of the most perfect unselfishness, of a devotion unalloyed by any thought of self. He went away for one moment to the window, and stood with his back to her, looking out unseeing on the blue hills and olive-clad slopes of the wide Val d'Arno.

She came up to him, her voice calm again.

'I am ready, Austen,' she said. 'We ought not to keep him waiting.'

Lord Austen left the room, and Marion stood waiting where he had left her.

CHAPTER XVII.

IT very seldom happens in real life that a long-expected event takes place in the way that might have been expected. Both Eustace and Marion had known that some day, and somewhere on earth, they should probably meet again, and both had thought with dread of that meeting—dread of its pain, of the surging misery of the past rising up again, and for the moment overwhelming everything in its force. The possibility of it had been a nightmare to both. And now the moment had come, and Marion's one thought was how to make this man, whom she had once loved so deeply, as happy as herself; and Eustace could think of nothing but the little, timid, gentle wife who was in the midst of such fearful danger, and away from his protection.

But as he opened the door, and saw her standing by the window, the blood rushed to his face and receded, leaving him deadly white. She was so wonderfully beautiful. Nothing in life could ever be to him what this peerless woman had once been.

Marion came forward with outstretched hands.

'We have news of Kitty,' she said.

He did not look at her. He held her hand, his bent head turned away. The words he would fain have uttered would not come to his dry lips.

She sat down quietly—her knees were trembling—and he stood in the same attitude before her, striving manfully to master himself.

'It is very wonderful what this Kitty of ours is doing,' she said, in that old familiar voice with the slight foreign accent. ' She, who is so young and small and tender, has given herself up to a work from which the very strongest and boldest have shrunk. I have seen something of cholera; it is very terrible. Kitty is all self-sacrifice.'

She looked up at him. He nodded his head in acquiescence. What should she say? For a moment her heart quailed within her. That he was suffering almost to the utmost limit of mental suffering, she felt and knew. Had she made a cruel mistake?. Was her fancied kindness only another wrong? Then a brave, unconventional thought came to her, and, with a quick prayer for help, she began to speak.

'Eustace,' she said, 'the time must have come, sooner or later, when we should meet again, and this first meeting must be strange, almost as if we had both died and met in another world. But the old past gives me a right to speak to you that without it I should not have had. . . . We have both suffered.'

Still he did not speak. He had raised his arm, leant it against the window-frame, and hidden his face upon it.

Her voice grew imploring now.

'Perhaps I have been cruel, Eustace; but I wanted to tell you, the old sorrow is healed now. If it were the same with you, I would thank God. I am very happy now.'

'I am glad.'

He spoke hoarsely. Any words were a relief.

She touched his shoulder very slightly.

'I think also you will be very happy, dear; for you will go to her, will you not? Your little wife, whose blue eyes have grown so wistful, so pathetic from watching for one sign of love from you! She loves you as only wives love their husbands; for you she would die. Nay, she has done more than that; because, in her longing to save you from pain, she broke her own heart and went away. You will not let her hunger like this all through this life that is so long?'

He raised his head; his lips were quivering still, yet he could face her now.

'I am going now—at once,' he said.

'God bless you, Eustace, and give her back to you. All will yet be well.'

A wonderfully radiant smile was on her face. Then he conquered himself with a strong effort, clearing the hoarse tone of his voice, and began to speak of Kitty's letter,

and how best he should fulfil her commissions. He determined to take all the
stores she required to Santa Chiara himself
that afternoon, and she undertook to get
them together while he returned to the
Hotel dell' Arno to break his intention
to his mother.

When Lord Austen came in after his
departure, Marion was quite unnerved, and
could not restrain her tears. For some
days he did not ask her to tell him what
had passed between them.

Eustace had to undergo passionate remonstrances and complaints from his
mother. She raved, varying her complaints with agonized entreaties, till he
did not know what to say to comfort
her, and convince her that nothing would
alter his fixed determination. Alice was
the greatest help to him. She looked upon
his plan as inevitable, in spite of the terror

with which it inspired her, and her restraining hand on his kept him silent. When in the midst of his mother's ravings she told him how Kitty had come to Florence, and how she had thought it right to give her a useful lesson and show her that she had proved herself so deep a disgrace to the family, Eustace controlled himself, but his heart burnt within him. He felt a remorse that amounted to agony that all this that had come upon Kitty was his doing. She, who had been so wonderfully generous, and noble, and loving, he had exposed to such treatment. He had failed utterly in his marriage vows, and every moment that she remained alone and under the impression that his mother had forced upon her, only added to his remorse a sense of guilt towards her.

He got away at last, leaving Lady Bellingham prostrate in a violent attack of hysterics, and by three o'clock he was in the train on the way to Santa Chiara.

The official of whom he demanded his ticket could not believe his ears.

'Santa Chiara!' he repeated. 'Surely not Santa Chiara?'

'Yes, yes; it is all right.'

'But I suppose the signore knows that once there he will not be able to leave again? There is a cordon round Santa Chiara which he cannot pass.'

'Nevertheless, I go,' said Eustace; and the man only shrugged his shoulders, with a feeling that no one on earth could account for the eccentricities of these Englishmen.

CHAPTER XVIII.

THE heat was frightful ; it seemed as if that day the horrors of that awful season had reached their height.

Marie di St. Isidoro, who hitherto had not been called upon to undertake any of the actual nursing, had at last been asked to help. Two of the Sisters had broken down, one from overwork, one from an accident, and they were short of hands. Dr. Menello had insisted upon their removal at once to a village near enough to be within the quarantine cordon, in hopes that a day or two of rest would restore their powers. Dr. Bruni had returned full of vigour and courage, but he was a man past sixty. The fatigue had told upon him, and he was not more than half rested. Menello was anxious that he should be spared night-work as much as possible.

And at last Marie was called upon to assist for a few hours. and enable the workers to rest. She was not of much use ; her delicate little white hands were almost powerless when she attempted the constant friction that was the only relief to many of the sufferers. She grew nervous and afraid to trust her memory in the punctual giving of medicines, and it was with tears of relief in her eyes that she found herself free at last to return home about seven o'clock in the evening. She thought of Kitty, so strong and indefatigable. In spite of her delicate, fragile looks, her activity and strength never flagged, and Marie felt humiliated that she could do so little, and very grateful for the few kind words of praise and thanks that Don Paolo gave her when she reached home.

Eustace arrived at the Palazzo St. Isidoro about ten minutes late. He had determined to go there first, imagining that in all probability he should find his wife there, or, at all events, information as to her whereabouts.

He found Marie alone, and when his name was first brought to her she failed to recognise it in its transmission through Italian lips, and she came to meet him as to an absolute stranger. Even when he advanced eagerly to shake hands she did not know him ; he was so far from her thoughts, and so much altered in appearance.

Seeing her polite, inquiring gesture, Sir Eustace for one moment hesitated, thinking that it was possibly intentional, and he began to introduce himself stiffly.

'You have forgotten me, madame,' he said. 'Will you let me recall myself to your recollection? I am Eustace Bellingham.'

Then Marie gave one of those little screams of delight that only Frenchwomen give, and threw up her hands.

'You have come! you have come at last!' she exclaimed. 'Ah, thank God, indeed!'

'Is my wife here?' he exclaimed, clasping the little white hand in both his. 'If she only knew how patiently I have sought her, and how I have despaired of ever finding her!'

'And how was it at last? Who told you?'

'A letter to Lady Austen. Lord Austen followed me to the station to tell me, only just in time.'

‘We heard that you had gone to the East.’

‘It was a mistake. I should never have gone so far out of reach of news. Will you not tell me where she is, and whether I may go to her at once ?’

‘I am afraid, greatly afraid, that you must be patient still. Kitty is at the hospital. You cannot go there—it is impossible ; and she will not be free before to-morrow morning. We are so short-handed.’

‘May I not even see her ? not tell her I am here ? Why should I not go to the hospital ? I have no fear.’

‘Ah! that is impossible,’ repeated Marie, with a shudder. ‘As to telling her, wait till Paolo comes in. I expect him every moment. Let us hear what he says.’

‘It is hard to wait,’ said Eustace feverishly ; but he agreed to do so. And as he sat by Marie he drew from her the whole history of Kitty's life since she had been at Santa Chiara, of her brave self-devotion, and the great talent for nursing and organization she had displayed.

Don Paolo came in presently, and his delight and thankfulness were so keen that a new light seemed to burst on Eustace as to the value and estimation in which his wife was held among her friends. During their long talk together that evening he perceived that Kitty was not the childish little clinging creature whom he had learnt to love for those very qualities, but a woman full of strength and power of devotion, unselfish and sweet—a character great enough in its perfect womanliness to deserve the name of ‘the little white Saint’ with which the people had endowed her.

Don Paolo thought that she ought not to be told of her husband's arrival that night. The work in the cholera-wards would be awful. He did not tell his guest so; but he, also, meant to return there immediately. Kitty would want all her powers to get through it. On the morrow they hoped for the arrival of four additional Sisters from Rome.

Just before they parted for the night, Eustace having been invited to sleep at Palazzo St. Isidoro, he asked the Priore to tell him what had become of Ursel.

Don Paolo never could well bear to speak of that story; but Eustace had a right to know—the right of strong affection for a mutual friend—and, with an effort at self-command, he told the whole story.

Eustace was deeply shocked. There was something about it that was fearfully tragical; and the former attempt at suicide seemed to leave little hope that the unfortunate musician might even now be alive somewhere. He felt that there could be little doubt that his mind had been unhinged by the shock of his misfortune.

When the Priore bade him good-night, they parted with a heavy sense of the great sorrow and mourning lying upon the world. Eustace threw himself on his sleepless bed, trying to think of future happiness, but totally unable to drive from his mind the terrible story of Ursel.

The next morning the Priore came into Eustace's room about six o'clock. He was excessively pale and worn-looking, but there was a smile on his face full of joy and congratulation.

'We always have Mass in the hospital chapel at seven o'clock,' he said. 'I thought you might like to be there. Your wife will be present; she always is. And then those who have been at the night-work go to bed. I don't know what you will feel about it. She ought to have her rest.'

Eustace was greatly disappointed, but he saw the truth of it.

'I shall, at least, see her in the chapel?' he said.

'Yes; and meet her after three o'clock. You will let me prepare her a little first, will you not?'

'Yes, that will be best. Can she come here?'

'My mother will fetch her at three, when you will find her quite revived and rested. Now let us start. I have changed my clothes, so I can take you across.'

'You have been up all night?'

'The work is heavy,' said Paolo gravely. 'But as I walked from the hospital this morning with Menello—the cleverest of our doctors—he spoke more hopefully. He does not think the disease quite so virulent in character. One or two cases have been quite mild, which is a good sign; and there are some hopeful cases of recovery. For instance, the poor fellow whom your wife has been especially nursing all through the night is really better this morning, and she is very sanguine.'

Eustace glanced at the sky; they had now emerged into the street.

'It does not look quite so cloudless as it did,' he said; 'but the heat in these close, overhung streets is tremendous.'

He thought so still more as they came into the piazza, with its stone pavement already hot underfoot, even at that early hour in the morning. Not a breath of air was stirring.

The little chapel of the hospital was dark and cool; the windows were all of stained glass. There was a division in it—a long, carved screen shutting off all the inmates of the hospital, with the Sisters, from the north side of the small nave, which was free to the public.

When Eustace came in, Don Paolo left him. He chose a quiet corner in which to place himself, and from thence, with a quick start, he recognised the form of his wife beyond the screen. She was kneeling, with her face hidden, quite motionless. The chapel bell outside kept up a sharp tang-tang.

The curtain before the door was pushed aside once or twice, and some one came in and knelt down. Presently a man, with a face both good and remarkable for its ex-pression of keen intellectual power, came in with a quick tread and took the chair next to Eustace. There was something about this man singularly attractive to the Englishman. White and worn as he looked from hard work and scanty sleep, his brown eyes were bright, his whole appearance full of vigour and energy. He joined in the service, singing and responding in a deep baritone voice; and he was one of the few communicants.

An instinct told Eustace that this must be the Menello of whom the Priore had spoken.

The service was full of peace and refreshment; the deep, musical tones of Don Paolo's fine chanting seemed to linger on the air.

When all had left, Eustace did not move, for he could still see Kitty's motionless figure absorbed in devotion. Long gold and red and purple lights fell on her from the windows, and rested round her on the white polished floor of the chapel.

Presently a black-robed Sister came back, softly said a few words to her, and they left the chapel together.

When Eustace came out into the glare of

the piazza outside, he found Don Paolo and Menello standing together. Menello accepted the introduction with cordial eagerness.

'It is good to see you!' he exclaimed. 'I am indeed rejoiced! I have been having a little argument with our friend here. He wished to leave our little white lady to sleep undisturbed; but I do not agree. She will sleep all the better for a little happiness.'

'But the shock of joy?'

'Ah, bah! It would seem as if you were the medical man and I the amateur. She is very strong; joy will help her. Why delay an hour, when we live, as we do, with our lives in our hands?'

The words made Eustace start, and realize the position he had almost forgotten more forcibly than ever.

Menello saw it.

'I forgot,' he said; 'you are not yet accustomed to such ideas. We are in the midst of a campaign.'

'Then I may see her at once?'

'Certainly! I will go and summon her to the visitors' room, where you can meet. I think we can do without her all day. The Roman Sisters will be here at half-past ten. Yes. You can take her back to Palazzo St. Isidoro; but you will see that she sleeps, will you not? It is necessary for her.'

'Yes, yes,' said Eustace eagerly, as he followed his conductor.

'I will wait here, you two impetuous boys!' said the Priore, turning back to the chapel. 'I want to speak to you, Ettore, when you can come.'

The visitors' room was a large, bare, whitewashed apartment, with a deal-table and benches running all round it; by the window a few chairs, and some pots of

flowers, which had all withered, and hung
black and dead on their stalks for want of
care and water.

Eustace found that he had to wait at least
ten minutes—and the time seemed endless.
Menello, though he had spoken of Kitty's
strength with confidence, and his conviction
that she could bear it well, knew thoroughly
what the shock of joy would be to one who
had lived so long in a twilight of sorrow ;
and it was with deep and skilful tenderness
that he slowly brought her mind to the con-
templation of possible happiness, and then
to the fact.

He did not know enough of her story to
understand why her joy was so full of
trembling, and how it was that when he
led her to the door she stood hardly able
to make up her mind to enter. It puzzled
him ; and he turned to seek the Priore
rather sorrowfully.

Kitty went in. Every kind of terror and doubt had assailed her. She hardly dared to raise her eyes. That bitter sense of shame, that in her busy life had altogether left her, rushed back with tenfold force. His mother's harsh words rang in her ears.

He came forward with one bound, and she was in his arms.

' My wife! My Kitty! have I found you at last? Oh, child, child! how could you leave me! Can you ever forgive me?'

It was all right. The bitter trembling doubts passed away for ever in the joy of that reunion.

She strove to beg his pardon for her own mistake; but he would not hear of it. It seemed as if all her task must be comforting him in his self-reproach, trying to make him forgive himself.

There were a thousand things to ask and

hear, but Eustace was inexorable—only one short hour would he allow himself and her: and then she must rest.

He told her that Menello had said that she could be spared most of that day; and she consented to return with him to Marie's house. Happy and radiant as she was, her soft blue eyes were almost closing with fatigue.

As they passed the chapel-door together, Menello touched Don Paolo's arm.

' I was right—you acknowledge it?' he said with a smile and a quick, sharp sigh.

They were so absorbed in each other that they did not perceive the two men who stood together under the porch. These had finished their business talk, when the Priore laid his hand on his friend's shoulder and said :

' I am glad you were able to come this morning, *Ettore mio.*'

'I also am glad,' he answered. 'In these days every Mass may be one's Viaticum!'

Don Paolo looked at him earnestly. He had spoken like that once or twice lately. But he looked well and strong; his brown eyes clear and lustrous.

'Ah!' he said with a sigh. 'Poor Bruni has not that help. These are days in which one feels most bitterly the misery of this modern freethinking.'

'Bruni is a splendid fellow,' said Menello quickly. 'Be at rest about him—he will not die; he will have time. But I must be gone. Somehow I have a feeling that the crisis is over. And look there!—a storm is coming! Ah! if it would but break! Think of the glory of a great rush of rain!' And his sigh was almost a gasp. 'Rain will be sweet and refreshing as hope and happiness and reunion!'

'Ah! your mind goes back to the joy of our little white lady.'

'Yes ; it is a good omen. The shades of night are breaking at last! Good-bye, Priore. If I can, I will look in late this evening.'

And he returned to his work. The Priore looked after him wistfully.

'A brave and singularly white soul!' he said to himself. 'He is like a son to me.'

CHAPTER XIX.

THE long hours of that hot day passed in a wonderful dreamy happiness to Eustace and his wife. To him, it was like a haven of rest after a terrible storm; to her, it was as if she had found her refuge again, and a joy that she had never dared to hope for : that at last her husband had learnt to love her ! It was a very gentle, reverent love. No longer the mere protecting tenderness for weakness and dependence ; but full of admiration, and with a great sense of gain and thankfulness—a far safer foundation for their future happiness.

When Kitty awoke from sleep about one o'clock, she found Eustace still watching her. He had never left her.

A little later, a message came from Menello to say that she would not be wanted before six o'clock; for he had made an arrangement to supply her place. So they were able to remain together through the afternoon.

The message, however, had given Eustace a little shock. He so longed now to take her out of danger; to fly with her at once; to shield her from all risk and all suffering. But it could not be. And very gently, but un-flinchingly, she showed it to him; so that he grew ashamed of his selfish instinct, and agreed to let her go.

The heat grew more and more oppressive.

About five o'clock a messenger came in

great haste to summon Kitty—her patient was worse! The fatal collapse had set in! There was not a moment to lose!

Eustace went with her to the hospital. The breathless atmosphere was overpowering; and a strange lurid glare was on the horizon.

'I shall come here for news late,' he said; 'perhaps about ten o'clock. Can I see you then?'

'Yes, at ten punctually. I will come to the visitors' room. Oh, this atmosphere must be fatal!'

'Kitty, Kitty, take care of yourself!' he exclaimed, in a tone of passionate entreaty. 'Darling, I could not lose you now!'

She did not answer save by one look as she went swiftly upstairs, and he turned away with a strange sinking at his heart.

Eustace felt that, in spite of the deadly

heat, he could not go indoors. His steps led him out on the Roman road, through the great gates of the town, up the long, dusty hill he knew so well—the familiar way to Ursel's house. He wanted to watch the great storm that was coming so rapidly on its way. The cholera cordon was outside the old restaurant. Beyond that cordon was no exit now.

He reached the top of the hill, and sat down to rest and regain breath on the same stone seat on which Kitty had sat when Ursel met with his fatal accident some weeks ago. Before him, range upon range, lay the blue Tuscan hills; the sky overhead heavy, leaden in hue like a mighty pall. In the far distance rolled the deep roar of thunder.

The storm, so long looked for, prayed for with such longing, was coming at last. Through the gathering darkness broke a fierce glare of lightning, and the roar came nearer up the valley. Flash after flash rent open the sky, and the thunder became incessant, the mighty chariot-wheels of the wrath of God.

Eustace sat still, watching with a strange fascination as the great storm came hurrying on. A line of fitful green light seemed to outline the mountains; then it broke straight overhead. The lightning blazed round him, great purple and green flames; the rattle and crash, as the huge thunder-clouds met, shook the very ground, the sound never ceasing. A sweeping blast of cold air rushed through the valley with a whistling sound, and as the whole heaven seemed torn open with one terrific glare, down came the rain in torrents. As if a river in the sky had burst its barriers, it poured down; it rushed along the ground, leaping up to meet the awful electric light, adding with the whistling dash of waters to the mighty din of heaven's tremendous artillery.

Eustace drew back under the portico of the restaurant. The house was closed. The pestilence had done its work there, and had left nothing more to do. He clung to the slight shelter as the storm tore and raged around, half-intoxicated by the grandeur and awfulness of the scene.

Suddenly, through the darkness and ever-increasing din he heard the sound of a human shout, and some one came reeling in against the doorpost, catching at him convulsively with a kind of laugh. He held the man fast, and the next sudden glare of purple light revealed to him close, in his very grasp, the figure of Ursel.

Neither spoke. They remained, as it were, locked together till the next vivid flash came, and they saw that their eyes were fixed on each other, fixed through the darkness—in Ursel's an awful look—wild, bloodshot.

He spoke first, the words shouted above the din :

' " The tendons of the wrist are severed; he will never play again!" '

' Ursel, dear Ursel!' cried Eustace. 'Take me to your house ; it must be close by. Ah, thank God we have met!'

' Too late!' cried Ursel, in the same wild voice. ' I have come over hill and dale; I have been racing the storm. They told me far away in the north that the storm would drive away the cholera ; and I have come to seek the cholera, to clasp it to my breast, if it will be kind to me and give me death! But I am too late—too late! The storm has won the race!'

Indescribably shocked, Eustace tried hard to open the door behind him, and by a vigorous thrust succeeded. He drew Ursel into the little empty place, with its marble tables and stone floor. He lit a match, and was able to find a rough lamp out of which the paraffin was not all gone; there was light enough to see Ursel's face. The unfortunate musician sat down passively, his head falling on his breast. Now and then he raised one hand and looked at it very curiously and pitifully; then he turned round to Eustace, and repeated in a voice which was all one cry:

'"The tendons of the wrist are severed; he will never play again!"'

The hot tears rushed to his friend's eyes.

'Dear Ursel,' he said, 'some day, when this sad life is over, your right hand will be well again, your old gift restored.'

'I am not too late?' he cried eagerly. 'I have raced the storm; the hills are far and very steep ; my boots are almost gone!' And he looked down on the torn and ragged shoes upon his feet   'And the storm has won the race. Let me go!' he shouted suddenly.   'I have not arrived yet. There may still be time. The storm is here ; perhaps it has not yet reached the town. Keep off ! Let me go!'

In vain Eustace held him ; with all his force he shook him off, and rushed out into the full wildness of the storm. The thunder clashed overhead with a splitting roar, and Eustace covered his face with his hands, commending the mad soul to God. After a few minutes that seemed interminable, the first fury abated, the rain settled down into one steady downpour, the thunder grew more sullen, and Eustace left the shelter, for which he had conceived an insurmountable horror, and with some difficulty found his way back to Palazzo St. Isidoro.

He found Don Paolo and Marie waiting for him in anxiety. At the first sight of his face Marie uttered a little scream.

' Ah! no more bad news!' she exclaimed. ' What has happened?'

There was no time to lose if any means were to be taken to try and find poor Ursel. Eustace told the story of what he had seen. It was strange to him to see Don Paolo's almost passionate burst of thankfulness; he, ordinarily so calm and self-contained, could not refrain from tears. To him the relief and gratitude were beyond all utterance.

In spite of the drenching rain and constant fresh outburst of tempest, the Priore, with one or two hastily-summoned assistants, started at once on their search. He and Marie prevailed on Eustace not to accompany them. He was wet through and shivering, and, moreover, their plan of search lay among streets and alleys not known to him, and, though they did not tell him so, into the very worst of the cholera haunts.

The hours passed by, they did not return, and at ten o'clock Eustace set out for the hospital. The storm had spent itself. It was like walking through a hot-vapour bath, pavement, houses—all steaming and reeking, the water rushing down the ill-paved streets in yellow rivers ; now and then up a side street a cold, chilly wind off the far-distant hills passing through, making him shudder as with the hot and cold rigor of ague.

He came in sight of the flaring lamp over the hospital-door, which lighted up with its yellow glare a statue of the patron saint, the gentle physician, St. Luke.

His ring was answered at once by a lay

Sister with a frightened, scared look on her face.

'Your wife has sent me,' she said, 'to ask you to wait in the visitors' room ; she cannot come at this moment.'

'And the patient she was nursing? He goes on well?'

'She has but now closed his eyes. Who could rally in such an atmosphere as this ?'

And the lay Sister shivered as she brought a chair and turned up the wick of the dim lamp upon the table.

'My wife is resting ?'

'No. There will not be much rest to-night. They have just brought in another patient, a terrible case, like those we had at first, that are, I am thankful to say, rarer now. This will not last long.'

'Then I shall not see her ?'

'If you can wait, maybe she will be able to spare you some minutes a little later.'

' Thank you very much.   I will wait any time.'

The good little woman nodded, and went away.   Eustace sat by the dim flickering lamp, resting his head on his hand, absorbed in thought.

The great bells of St. Onofrio in the distance clanged out hour after hour, but there was no sign of Kitty.

Eustace made himself as comfortable as he could, leant his head against the wall, and, worn out by the continued agitations of the day, fatigue triumphed over discomfort, and he slept.

He did not know how long that sleep lasted, but he was aroused by a gleam of light, and, opening his eyes, he saw two figures standing before him—Don Paolo in the shadow, with a very solemn, grave look on his face ; his young wife holding a lighted candle high above him, her sweet, serious face illuminated so that she looked like some white sacred statue on the dark background.

Eustace sprang to his feet.

' You have come at last!' he exclaimed. Then to the Priore, ' You also?   Tell me how you have prospered.'

' I thought Sister Agata had told you,' said Kitty softly.   ' Poor Ursel was brought in about nine o'clock.'

' You found him?'

' Yes,' said the Priore mournfully, ' I found him.   It is one of the worst attacks of Asiatic cholera ; it is very awful.'

' Is there hope?'

Don Paolo looked at Kitty, and she shook her head.

' You could not desire life for him,' she said.

' It is best as it is.'

' And surely,' said Eustace earnestly,

'this awful suffering will expiate his sins?'

'Surely, surely,' said Don Paolo, clasping his hands together.

A Sister came in.

'You are wanted,' she said to Kitty; 'Dr. Menello wants you at once.'

Kitty turned to her husband.

'You will go home now, Eustace, will you not?' she said. 'Indeed, you can do no good here.'

'May I not see him?'

'No, no. Were it to any purpose it would be your duty, but you can do nothing. He would not know you.'

Very reluctantly he let her go, and, at the Priore's strong representation that nothing could be so bad for Kitty as unnecessary risk on his part, allowed himself to be persuaded to go home.

He was back at the hospital at five o'clock

the next morning. The air was freshened and sweetened by the rain to an extraordinary extent. He revelled in its cool dampness ; there was a life in it that had been wanting for many a long, weary day.

Life, too, seemed to have revived in the hospital. The stairs were being washed—dusting, sponging, freshening going on ; the lay Sister who took him into the visitors' room was quite gay. Some of the patients were so much better. One young girl, whose life had been despaired of in the fatal collapse, had taken a turn about midnight, and was much better.

' And Ursel ?'

' Ursel — who is that ? Oh, number forty-eight ; I remember. Oh ! he is a lost man ; but it is the will of God. The cramps are very bad ; he is in a private room. They say he has been sensible. Dr. Menello was with him most of the night.

Bruni is there now, and Dr. Menello has gone to the women's wards. He will be cheered by the sight of little Giuseppina ; it will do him good!'

She chattered on.

Eustace walked restlessly up and down the room. The hours passed ; then a little pencilled note was brought to him, which he could hardly decipher :

'Have patience, darling ; I will come as soon as I can.'

But Kitty came not. He returned to the Palazzo St. Isidoro for pens and paper, which he took to the hospital, and set himself to letter-writing with all his power; and the hours passed, and it was once more afternoon.

At last the door was pushed open, and Kitty came in, followed by both the Priore and Menello. There was a worn, exhausted look on their faces. Kitty alone did not look so much exhausted as radiant. She came straight up to her husband.

'It is all well with him,' she said. 'It is over.'

'Was he sensible?' asked Eustace; and Don Paolo answered:

'For one short hour; but it was enough. He held my hand in one brief interval of rest from that death-agony, and I heard his words just breathed:

'"*Fiat voluntas Tua.*" Thank God! Thank God!'

He covered his face with his hands.

Then Kitty, without sign or warning, suddenly grew white as snow, and fainted away in a long swoon in her husband's arms.

CHAPTER XX.

THE next morning passed, and noon, with all its tempered freshened heat, and still Kitty Bellingham slept. The house was kept perfectly silent ; all the meals and necessary business were carried on downstairs. She was completely exhausted. Eustace sat by her without moving. Dr. Menello came in once, tried her pulse, smiled well satisfied, and only bade them leave her alone.

' " The little white lady is under the protection of the angels," they say at the hospital,' he said. 'Leave her to her guardians.'

The long sleep, the awakening to perfect happiness, all revived her wonderfully. For two or three days Menello made her rest, after which she resumed her work with renewed vigour.

'It is so easy now, and so glorious to see the people getting well!' she exclaimed one day. 'The worst is all over, Marie dear.'

'Ah! and now you will soon be leaving us,' said Madame di St. Isidoro. 'Your husband has been wonderfully good and patient—but, alas! you are no longer indispensable; others can do your work, and there will be no excuse for lingering here.'

'Eustace has been very patient,' said Kitty, smiling. 'To-day he was beginning to talk of where we shall go to get through our quarantine; and then——'

' Home?'

'Not yet ; he has a fancy for another honeymoon—a long *tête-à-tête* somewhere before we settle down again.'

' Then you start soon?'

She had not thought that it was so near, and the tears rushed to her eyes.

' Eustace talked of Monday,' said Kitty rather falteringly. ' The Roman Sisters do all the work now.'

' Monday? Ah, well! so it must come. You will take the sunshine of the place away with you.'

Kitty threw her arms round her neck, kissing her again and again.

That evening Menello came to Don Paolo, and asked him to walk with him.

' I want to get out on to the fortification on the west side of the town,' he said. ' I want to feel the sweet fresh air on the grass slopes there. I have a little patient to visit close by—a baby whose mother died of the cholera ; it is thriving under a very kind, gentle little goat, that nurses it like its own kid; and the baby is such a nice sunny little thing that it always refreshes me to see how well it goes on. The poor father loves it dearly.'

The two friends walked together up the green slopes that led to the fortifications. The baby, as usual, was lying on the grass outside its home, the goat browsing close by; a very old crone sat knitting coarse yarn, and crooning to them both.

Menello knelt down by the baby and played with it a little while ; the child knew him well, looked up in his face, pulled his long moustaches, and crowed with delight.

When he rose and joined Don Paolo, the answering sweetness of his smile lingered yet upon his lip.

Over the far horizon the sun was going down in a magnificent blaze of glory: the distant hills, the deeply-shadowed plain, the grass on which they stood, were bathed in a golden glow.

Slowly, from right and left, great ink-purple clouds came sailing up, each as it approached touched with crimson fire—relentless, irresistible, with mighty doors closing round the dying monarch.

The glow faded—a still, gray twilight stole over the world; in the west lingered a long blood-red streak of light, and far away the topmost peaks of the marble mountains shone clear, transparent as the gleam of rose-colour upon crystal, dying out one by one into shadow.

Menello watched it all in silence; then, still holding his friend's arm, they turned towards the town.

'The sun will rise on another world,' he

said; ' and Ursel's sun has risen where he will have learnt how discord is turned into harmony.'

' Requiescat in pace!' said the Priore softly. Looking up into his friend's face, he was struck by a strange gray colour in it he had never seen before. ' Ettore!' he exclaimed, in a sudden cold terror, ' you are not well! What is it?'

' Let us get to the hospital,' he answered. ' Do not tell the little white lady. It will soon be over!'

' What is it? Ettore! Oh, my boy! my more than son!'

He smiled a strange forced smile.

They were at the gates now, and by rare good fortune found a carriage and were driven to the hospital.

They helped him out on to the hospital steps. There he stood for one moment looking up at the sky. Two or three little

clouds still lingered, touched with rosy
light. Then suddenly he threw out his
arms with a short cry of mortal agony,
and they carried him in and shut the door.

Day and night, day after day, the crowd
gathered round the hospital-door, women
and men alike with streaming eyes, hanging
upon the news from within, where Life and
Death battled with frightful force for their
idol.

And on the sixth day, as the crowd, in
tumultuous anxiety, swarmed round the
hospital, the great bell of St. Onofrio began
to toll solemnly, and an old Sister, with
the tears pouring down her face, came out
upon the steps and told the sobbing, moan-
ing people that the noble, pure young soul
had gone Home.

They received the news at first almost
with incredulity. How could it be that
one on whom they all had learnt to depend

so entirely—so strong, so vigorous, so over-
flowing with life and energy—should be cut
off like this, hardly yet in the prime of
life?

The cry and wail that rose from the
crowd re-echoed down the street; one after
another took up the bitter tidings and
swelled the torrent of lamentation.

Don Paolo, as he walked home from the
hospital, had on his face a stricken look, as
if the shadow of Death had passed over
him and withered him into age. For once
he had no words of comfort to give to the
sobbing men and women who pressed round
him; the physical power of uttering them
had left him. He could only creep home
to fight out his battle by himself in solitude
and prayer.

Eustace and Kitty lingered on yet for
some days at Santa Chiara. They could
not bear to leave their friends in the first

hours of their grief. But the time came at last, and they were obliged to go.

The dreaded cholera had done its worst, and now every day showed improvement; anxious nursing gave way to care for convalescents. The great heat of that awful autumn passed away, and the fresh cold of a healthier season set in.

Groups of careworn men used to stand every day looking down into the deep marble basin of the Bruzzi fountain, watching how daily the water rose and promised soon to flow in its former rich abundance.

On one soul, Ettore's life and death, in all the power of their strength and goodness, had an undying result.

It was one of the first gleams of joy which came to refresh the grief-worn Priore, when one evening—when long shadows were dimming the dark aisles of St. Onofrio—

Bruni, the clever, self-sufficient, intellectual man of science, came to him asking:

'What shall I do to be saved?'

CHAPTER XXI.

'PAOLO,' said Marie di St. Isidoro to her son one day about Easter in the following year, 'I have just received a long letter from Alice Bellingham, containing all the news of our friends that we were hoping to hear.'

'I am glad,' said the Priore. 'May I see it?'

Marie put it into his hand, and turned away to attend to the blooming pots of purple and white violets in the windows —which were again her especial delight— while he read it.

'My dearest Marie,

'It was very good of you to write
to me such a long and interesting letter;
and I will try and answer all the questions
you ask me without forgetting any. But
it is a little difficult to write, for May is
singing, and it is so wonderfully beautiful
that it charms away one's senses. Kitty is
accompanying her—she says no one ac-
companies like Kitty.

'I think you would be satisfied with us
all now. Eustace and Kitty are perfectly
happy. He is devoted to her, waiting
on her as if she were the most fragile piece
of Dresden china, instead of the strong
dependable character we know her to be.
There is something wistful in his devotion
to her—as if the remembrance of the past
were still strong. She is the most altered
of the two; she has quite lost the timidity
that used to oppress her so much, and is at

her ease, with a pretty dignity all her own.

' Mrs. Brown-Clifford has returned to her house—sister, cats and all. She never goes to Castleford, but little Kitty often goes to her, and Eustace also—oddly enough, I think he is quite fond of her. In fact, Kitty has won everyone. Mamma is so very fond of her now—ever since the day when she went to see her at Georgie's house, very nervous as to what she might say, and afraid of a breach between herself and Eustace, and found dear Kitty only ready to rush into her arms and ask for forgiveness herself, instead of giving it. Mamma was quite won over. In fact, Kitty might well be spoilt if she were not unspoilable from the wonderful sweet humility which is her greatest charm.

' That photograph you sent to her is quite beautiful. I found Kitty in her boudoir crying over it as if her heart would break ;

and I could not make out who it was till Eustace showed me the name, "Ettore Menello," in the Priore's handwriting. She never speaks about the cholera-time—that end to it was too terrible! and Eustace asked us not to speak about it. He has told me something of it, and of Ursel's death.

'When will you fulfil your promise and come to England? I think Eustace and Kitty would be even more perfectly contented than they are if they could welcome you here, and Don Paolo, to whom they say they owe more than words can express.'

Don Paolo put down the letter.

'We could wish for nothing better than that account,' he said, smiling. 'I am very glad.'

Marie hesitated a little; then she said:

'And this invitation?—it is so often

repeated. Do you think, Paolo, that some day we could go?'

'Yes, some day, when I have time,' said the Priore.

'But when will that be?'

'Ah! when?' he answered with a smile.

THE END.

BILLING & SONS, PRINTERS, GUILDFORD
G., C. & Co.